SIDEWAYS

Sideways

LISA HUGHEY

Speakeasy
TAPROOM

HeartEyes
Press

1

TRACY

"Get out of town."

Tracy Thayer fumbled with her cell phone, staring blearily at the time. It was six a.m.

"Who is this?" Her voice was raspy. She didn't typically get up this early. Who the hell was calling her this early in the morning?

"It's Bernie." Bernie Montague was the communications director for her father's congressional office. And her boss.

Her boss?

Tracy rolled onto her back and sank into the luxurious thousand-count Egyptian cotton sheets while she tried to make sense of what he was saying. "You want to repeat that?"

"Not particularly." He sounded pissed.

Tracy tended to wake up slowly. A morning person she was not. Especially since she'd been up late consoling her brother over his broken engagement. "What's wrong?"

"Reporters got ahold of a news story about you."

"Me?" She was the picture of responsibility. She never did anything to jeopardize her family's standing.

"A dating app, Tracy? Really?"

Oh shit. Except for that. Shock rendered her mute. No one was supposed to know about the app. No one. Even her best friends—with the exception of Pete Nguyen and his girlfriend, Britt, who had worked on the technical details—had no idea she'd developed a dating app. Her heart began a rapid tattoo.

Her family didn't know. Her father was a politician, long-standing in the House of Representatives, like his father before him. And her brother was currently running for state office.

She knew enough about the media to know this wasn't a good thing. No reason to pretend ignorance. "How did they find out?"

"We don't have time for this."

She wasn't sure why it was so urgent.

Bernie began to rant. "A secret? You of all people know how damaging a secret can be."

"I was trying to protect everyone. You'll be able to spin this."

"If I had known about it and had a month or two to plan, with a detailed talking points memo, but right now we're in strict damage-control mode. You need to get out of town before the vultures start circling. Luckily I got a heads-up from a friend at the Globe."

Tracy shoved to sitting and swung her feet to the floor. "Why do I need to leave?"

She had media training. She worked part time in her father's office in Boston doing marketing and social media. She could help.

"We need to craft a statement and get the messaging exactly correct," Bernie said. "Right now, we need you inaccessible. No comment until we nail it down."

She couldn't do that from her condo?

"Just take off for the weekend. Jesus Christ. I still have to break this to your father."

Her father got up early every morning and took a long walk on the grounds of their family estate in Wellesley. He should be having his morning breakfast, oatmeal with cinnamon and dried cranberries and walnuts, and a single hard-boiled egg, right now. If he had the television on, he was about to be shocked.

"It's not like I killed someone." As she woke up more, she was starting to get more pissed.

"Damage control, babe." Bernie sighed. He sounded tired.

"Where do you want me to go?"

"Someplace no one will think to look for you." She could hear Bernie pacing his home office. "Rent a car under an alias and lie low. Turn off your cell. Call me on Monday from one of your burners."

He was taking this pretty seriously.

Her throat closed and she curled into a ball. What would her father think about it all? He was up for reelection and his opponent had been trying to make something dirty stick to her father for months.

She had the means to deliver a blockbuster exposé about her well-known political family. Not that she ever would.

The irony wasn't lost on her.

But that would have to wait for later. Right now, she needed to get the hell out of Dodge.

She threw a couple pairs of khaki crop pants and washable silk button-up blouses into her traveler suitcase. Ballet flats, a small case of Tiffany casual jewelry, and her overnight cosmetic case. She grabbed her small emergency wallet which included a thousand dollars cash, a debit card, a burner phone, and a fake ID.

She thought about the situation and went to her safe. She pulled out an ID she'd never used before. Cee-Cee. Her imaginary persona. The one she'd created when she was a teenager and wished for a different life.

Some kids had imaginary friends.

Tracy had created an imaginary identity.

She'd never used Cee-Cee before but instinctively she tossed it in her Balenciaga bag—having her secret come out without the benefit of spin ahead of time could be the catalyst to finally bring Cee-Cee to life. She'd always hesitated but the alarm in Bernie's voice had been surprising. He was usually unflappable. His brain worked in twenty directions at once, always coming up with the perfect spin, so him freaking out about this was a big fat clue that it was bigger than she expected.

Being the daughter of a politician, she'd gotten used to traveling under aliases when the occasion demanded it. Perhaps this time she could become Cee-Cee.

Her doorbell buzzed.

Tracy frowned. She lived in a building with high security. She peered through the security hole. Shit.

A reporter she'd had drinks with a few months ago was on her doorstep. He'd dropped her home after their date. She didn't even know why she'd gone out with the guy. Reporters were necessary tools in the political world but having a relationship with one was a bad idea. Although she didn't think that was why he'd asked her out, she also knew that he'd use their connection to his advantage if the opportunity presented itself.

Only one dating option was worse than a reporter. Someone high profile and sought after by the press.

Too many opportunities for conflicts of interest. Too many possibilities that reporters would follow them and inadvertently reveal something about Tracy or her family. Some politicians courted the press but not the Thayers.

And she had a secret that would surprise everyone.

Fortunately, thinking on her feet was a strength. She dialed quickly then winced when the phone was answered groggily. It wasn't even seven a.m.

"Hey, I need a favor."

"Whatever you need." Britt Jones, who had started out as her pal Pete's girlfriend but was now her friend too, didn't even hesitate.

"That fast?" Tracy was overwhelmed with emotion.

"I just got a check from the profit sharing." Britt laughed huskily. "Who knew digital dating was so profitable."

Tracy had built a multimillion dollar dating empire, but she hadn't gone on a third date in years. Too afraid of the consequences of falling in love with someone and too much longing for a partner who she could never be truly honest with.

"Well, enjoy, because apparently it's out that Fairy Tale Beginnings is mine." Tracy fiddled with her Tiffany charm bracelet, fingering the princess crown. A gift from her mother. "New Wins may be getting some media calls."

She wouldn't think that the information that she was the owner would be bad. After all, she had a kickass CEO, and the programming behind the app was top-notch.

"We didn't have anything to do with a breach."

"I know that." Pete had had an employee theft issue last summer, but he'd been quick to fix the problem without too much fanfare and as far as she knew there hadn't been any recent issues.

There was a pause on the other end. "You didn't think it could stay private forever, did you?"

She'd actually hoped she could keep it a secret forever. "No, but I would have preferred to control the rollout and the message." She should have had a plan in place for when the information got out. That was on her. She had a few talking points available but that was it. Instead of being proactive, she had hidden her head in the sand and pretended that it wouldn't get out, and if it did it wouldn't be a big deal.

"What happened?"

"Still not sure. But I've been ordered to get out of town for a few days."

"Get out of town?" Britt paused. Tracy could practically hear her shaking her head. "Rich people."

Tracy laughed. "Political people."

"What do you need?"

"Can you rent a car and drive it to my building? I'll meet you in the parking garage on the second floor."

When she'd bought her condo, she'd picked a unit that had a back access to the service elevators. That would certainly come in handy today.

"Done. See you in a few minutes."

"You're a lifesaver!"

Britt showed up half an hour later with Pete. Peter Nguyen was one of her close-knit group of friends who'd met when they were in their late teens and formed an oddball group of people with nothing in common except the ambition to become billionaires.

What started out as an incongruous group of diversely different people had developed into a friendship bond that grew stronger every year.

Pete and Britt were old high school friends who had reconnected last summer. They'd fallen in love while doing the software development of Tracy's app. Maybe she, and Fairy Tale Beginnings, had had a slight hand in getting them together. Unless Pete had cheated and programmed the app to match him with Britt. Tracy was never sure if that was the case.

They had just gotten engaged and were deliriously happy, as evidenced by the fact that he'd come with Britt this morning.

Pete said, "Do you need anything else from us?"

"I'm going to hole up somewhere and figure out where the leak came from."

"You've got me on speed dial." Pete was clearly lost in details as he rattled off his next moves. "I'll run a diagnostic and make sure we didn't have a security breach. Although if we did, my threat detection program should have caught someone trying to hack the system."

"My guess is that someone somewhere figured it out."

She needed to call her CEO, Yolanda Sanchez, and get a statement crafted. She'd wait until Bernie released his, so that there weren't any contradictions between the two. But they should at the very least have a draft ready to go.

Yolanda had been with Tracy since the beginning. She was one of the few people who knew that Tracy was the owner and creator of Fairy Tale Beginnings. They'd become friends over the past year.

Tracy had set up a shell company, legally, that owned Fairy Tale Beginnings. So someone would have had to find the filing documents for her shell company. She'd used a different lawyer, not her family attorney, to set it up and the ownership filings were secret. The laws had just changed so the information was going to come out sooner or later.

She just wished it had been later.

Up until now she'd been able to keep her identity private. She was just about ready to file paperwork for two new businesses, offshoots spawned by the original company. The largest was an engagement-planning business that helped clients design spectacular announcements and over-the-top proposals worthy of Instagram and TikTok. They helped their clients plan amazing events.

Something weird that she'd never really anticipated. She'd always thought that such an intimate moment should be just that, intimate. But plenty of people craved the spotlight, wanting their fifteen minutes of fame and the possibility of going viral. And she and her company knew how to deliver.

Now she had an Instagram feed just for proposals from people who were matched using her app. And another Instagram account strictly for wedding photos of Fairy Tale marriages.

She needed to check in with Yolanda and see if there was any backlash from the users of the app. She could also do a search online. But all that would have to wait until she got away from the reporters congregated outside her building.

"Thanks for your help." Tracy squeezed Pete and then Britt in tight hugs. "Can you tell the BBC?" Yes, she was a chickenshit.

Her friends from the Billionaire Breakfast Club—that silly name they had coined all those years ago—were going to be annoyed with her.

She'd kept things from them. Kind of big things. But she'd had reasons. Namely protecting her family. And they'd think the app was silly.

Even her brother, who'd used the app to find Esme, his ex-fiancée, thought it was dumb. But he'd been tired of women who'd been attracted to him strictly because of his family name. He'd been searching for a woman of a certain background who was ready to be in the spotlight. Tracy had been the one to suggest he try it. He was going to be doubly pissed since Esme had broken it off yesterday.

She wore sunglasses and her floppy beach hat. Her hands gripped the steering wheel hard. Tracy drove out of the garage past the small circle of reporters waiting outside. Fortunately, they were so intent on the front door, that they missed her leaving.

So cray. Hopefully this would all blow over in a day or two and she'd be back in the city. But where to escape for a few days? She hopped on the Mass Pike and headed inland. Away from the city. Away from her life. Away from her problems.

She stopped in a large suburban town with a plethora of strip malls and picked up a new smart phone. She'd set it up later. Her go bag would hold her over for the next few days but she needed access to the internet.

Hours later, after wandering the backroads, she'd traveled into Vermont.

She was a city girl. She must have been to Vermont at some point in her twenty-nine years, but she couldn't recall when.

Which meant no one would think to look for her here.

An hour later, she pulled off the road and went in search of some lunch. After a bit, she happened upon a sign for the Speakeasy Taproom.

The name conjured up visions of an illicit underground bar.

She loved the symbolism—hiding out in a den of ill repute where no one would think to look for Boston heiress Tracy Thayer.

She'd stop here.

The old mill building had been restored. Giant, leaded glass windows broke up the brick exterior giving her a glimpse inside. Tracy paused near the door and changed course, heading to the little area to the left of the entrance. Around the back was an outdoor patio that bordered the rushing river. The birds twittering and the swishing of wind through the trees were unfamiliar pastoral sounds. She was more used to honking horns and the chatter of thousands of people hurrying to get on with their day.

Even with the sounds of nature, there was a hushed quality to the air, an expectant energy but without that crisp intensity of the city, more blurred like a watercolor scene. She paced the grassy area as her brain went over the events of this morning. She'd had nothing but time to think on her drive, and she was no closer to grasping what had happened and what was going on than when she'd been abruptly awoken this morning.

Tracy couldn't stand it any longer. She pulled out her burner flip phone and dialed her brother, Thomas. He didn't answer. Ugh. He wouldn't recognize the number. She left a message anyway. "Hey, what's going on? Call me back at this number."

She tried Bernie. But he didn't answer either.

She called her father. His personal assistant, Ashley, answered. "Congressman Thayer has no comment at this time."

"Wait, Ashley. It's Tracy."

"Oh my God. You were behind the Fairy Tale Beginnings? I used that app! I had to put the ten grand registration fee on a new credit card."

She wondered randomly why Ashley didn't pay cash for her registration fee. But she didn't have the time to ask. "Can you put me through to my father?" She needed information and she hated feeling out of the loop.

"Uh, he's in a strategy meeting right now. Can I take a message? Where are you?"

"Not important." Bernie's lessons followed her. "What about my brother? Is he around?"

"Also in the meeting since it involves him."

It involved her brother? Now she was totally confused.

"Pretty much everyone who needs damage control is in your father's office." Ashley sighed. "But it's closed-door so I have no idea what's going on."

"Give me the Cliff's Note version of the problem."

"Your brother's fiancée just left him – via tabloid – and said that the app lied about him and his values. And then she outed you."

How in the world had Esme, short for Esmerelda, found out Tracy was behind Fairy Tale Beginnings? Even her family didn't know. And what was her end game with outing her? Was she strictly a disgruntled ex or was there more going on here?

Esme had attacked her brother's values. Had Thomas told her about their family secret?

She had so many questions.

She hadn't like Esme from the get-go. There had been a calculated hardness in her gaze when they'd first met. But Tracy had let her reservations slide—she was naturally suspicious—because Fairy Tale Beginnings had matched them. And she had complete faith in her app.

She paced the uneven dirt area, her Tiffany bracelet sliding over her arm, charms tinkling against each other as she fought the urge to run her fingers through her hair.

"Can I have them call you back at this number?" A note in Ashley's voice set Tracy's alarm sensors blaring. Leaks weren't unheard of and while this was only the beginnings of a scandal, a dumb one at that, Ashley wouldn't be the first aide to try to cash in with the tabloids. Her father vetted his staff very carefully but sometimes his employees couldn't resist the lure of making money by selling Thayer family details.

Her family had been a subject of media interest for years. It was tiring—but an inexorable fact of her life.

A Help Wanted sign in fancy script rested in the front window. Waitressing in rural Vermont. She sighed. That would certainly be an easier life than her complicated tangle right now.

"I'll call back later."

She jabbed the button on her phone to hang up and then swore creatively. "Dammit. You should have known this would happen. You big dummy."

She mentally took it back. That wasn't her. She was always positive and upbeat, even when the world was on fire.

2

COLT

Colton Vega shifted uncomfortably in the booth at the Speakeasy Taproom and wished he were anyplace else on earth.

Nope, he took that back. He never wanted to work in a kitchen again—which is what his two old friends from culinary school were trying to convince him to do.

He was an asshole.

"Come on, Colt," Phoebe Stevens wheedled. She had recently relocated to Colebury and was the current head chef at the Speakeasy.

"We need you," Audrey Shipley chimed in. She'd come here a few years ago after finishing culinary school, met a local farmer and cider maker, and left Boston for the boonies of Vermont.

He leaned back in the rustic booth and raised an eyebrow at the two of them with a mixture of disbelief, annoyance, and yes, affection. "This town is lousy with high-quality chefs. You don't need me."

"I'm already swamped," Phoebe said. "And now that we're planning to expand and use the upstairs for events, we need a catering chef."

His stomach grinded. He hadn't stepped foot back in a kitchen since he'd had a complete meltdown on live television almost a year ago.

They really didn't know what they were asking. Or maybe they did...but still.

"Alec is hiring a catering manager. You won't have to interact with anyone. You just need to come in on event day and cook."

Alec Rossi, Audrey's brother-in-law, was part owner and a stand-up guy. On the surface it sounded easy. Just *cook*.

But there were so many emotions mixed in with going back into the kitchen. Feelings he never wanted to have again. Stress and addiction and hurting people he loved were all tangled up in the simple act of going back into the kitchen and cooking.

"I can't."

He hated the look of disappointment on their faces. Phoebe and Audrey wore similar expressions both determined and sweet.

"I really do appreciate everything you've done for me." He didn't want either of them to think he was ungrateful. He wasn't.

"Good friends look out for each other," Audrey said. "You would do the same for me."

But he knew that wasn't true. Colt's gaze shot around the renovated old mill building. The rough-hewn wood floors, brick walls, and old post and beam ceilings had a casual charm that was homey and eclectic.

The menu mimicked the atmosphere. Casual, hip, and not trendy but full of interesting and unusual flavor combinations. Phoebe had outdone herself but he expected nothing less than perfection from her. She'd been a successful chef in New York, working toward opening her own restaurant until her boyfriend and business partner had taken her idea and dumped her in public. The entire horrible moment had been caught on someone's phone, been posted on social media, and went viral.

Her situation was embarrassing, no question. But she hadn't hurt anyone. Not like Colt.

"Which is why we," Audrey and Phoebe glanced at each other,

then Audrey continued, "think getting back into the kitchen would be good for you."

He hated to let his friends down but going back into the kitchen was a bad idea.

"Hell, no." Just thinking about working in a kitchen again made him crave a hit of nicotine and a shot of Lagavulin 16.

He couldn't go back to the way he was in his past. He'd hurt everyone he loved.

"This wouldn't be like before."

He snorted. "You don't know that."

"I know you. You are a brilliant chef." Audrey patted his hand.

Some days he wasn't even sure he knew himself. So he wasn't sure how Audrey could be so sure.

She'd said "you *are* a brilliant chef." Maybe at one time he had been, but not now.

"Maybe I was." He no longer cooked anything other than scrambled eggs. It was safer for everyone if it stayed that way.

"You could do this in your sleep," Audrey said. "I found a permanent home here and I just want you to do the same."

His only goal right now was to stay healthy. Beyond that his life's desire involved not having goals. He never wanted to get back on that treadmill of long days and blind ambition.

"Today we'll just enjoy a yummy lunch with friends. Take a few days to think about it." Phoebe smiled. "I want you guys to try this new grilled cheese on the menu. The duck confit really makes it."

He might not cook anymore, but he still loved to eat. "Bring it on."

They let their pleas drop. Thank God.

A woman who looked like she'd come straight from shopping on Newbury Street made her way into the Speakeasy and sat at the high-top table behind them. Her clothes were the city version of casual and nowhere near what people in the country considered appropriate. Her blond hair was styled into a perfect shiny bob that framed her heart-shaped face, with high aristocratic cheekbones and plump lips that were pressed into a flat line.

Her nails matched the lipstick on her unsmiling mouth as she perused the menu. A tiny frown crinkled her perfectly crimped dark blond eyebrows.

Colt was unaccountably annoyed by the rich woman. He'd heard her on the way in, swearing at someone on the phone. Although it had been PG rated, her tone had been one of pure disgust. She was every white girl with an entitled attitude.

"What's wrong?" Phoebe studied him.

"The customer behind you annoys me." He didn't keep his voice down and the woman's startled gaze lifted to his. Her eyes were a brilliant cobalt blue. Dark like the perfect Maine blueberries that he'd used in his seared pork loin with a blueberry and mustard barbeque sauce. That dish had catapulted him into a James Beard award winner.

Her perfect pink lips formed an O and her brows lifted. She gave him a sunny smile. For a moment her warmth spread over him and he wanted to bask in her approval.

But he shoved away that desire for acceptance.

Heading down that path, looking for validation from others, would only lead to misery and disaster. She represented every wealthy patron he'd curried favor from in his quest to become a world-renowned premier chef. And he was self-aware enough to realize that when he lashed out at her he was really lashing out at himself—at least, his former self.

Besides, he didn't want or need her approval.

He studied her slender form and perfect appearance. She was probably like every constantly-on-a-diet woman who came into his restaurant and wanted to change his creations. Back then he'd been considered amusingly temperamental, so patrons put up with his mini rants about changing the flavors and composition of a dish and destroying the chef's vision.

Why go to a gourmet restaurant if you weren't going to eat the food the way the chef intended it to be eaten?

He could feel his temper rising, but he forced himself to relax and let it go.

Then he said to Audrey and Phoebe, "See, I'd be terrible at it. I'm already getting annoyed with customers and having to hold back from berating them." But that wasn't the only reason. The hoppy scent of Phoebe's Goldenpour IPA hit his nose. His mouth watered and he eyed the caramel liquid.

"You want a taste?" Phoebe had noticed his interest. "The Giltmaker family brews this." They were among the partners who owned the Speakeasy along with Griff, Audrey's husband, Alec Rossi, and Alec's uncle, Otto.

Maybe he could just have a sip.

And maybe he'd be headed to rehab.

Besides, his drink of choice had been Lagavulin. It had started with one glass at the end of the night to rewind after a sixteen-hour day.

But a few years in, he'd been starting the evening dinner shift with a glass of wine that turned into a bottle or two by the time the night was over. Then he'd move on to scotch. At that point, he'd be too hammered to appreciate the gorgeous amber color and the smoky peat flavor.

"Nah, I'm good." His friends had no idea that he'd been abusing alcohol. He'd had a strict no-drugs policy at his restaurants. Cocaine was common among the restaurant crowd, but he'd known enough people who had drug problems to ban it. That truth had been a crutch he'd used to justify his drinking—*at least I'm not doing cocaine.*

That intense pressure had decimated his life. His quest to achieve perfection had almost killed him and destroyed not only his career, but his life and family.

He never wanted to go back into the kitchen and risk his family and friends again.

TRACY

What a quaint little place.

Tracy sat at a high-top table on a tall stool and admired the brick walls, the twinkly lights and the mismatched antique lamps hanging from the ceiling. It was a far cry from Ostra, where she ate last Friday night with friends, with its throngs of waitstaff and artistic food presented with a theatrical flourish in an avant-garde atmosphere.

The rustic interior of the Speakeasy had a certain charm.

Except for the grumpy guy at the next table, who for some unknown reason didn't seem to like her, everyone had been friendly.

Tracy studied the three people at the table in front of her. Speculating about strangers was better than worrying about her own problems.

Two women and a man. She watched their body language, unable to turn off the neuroscience analytics that convinced her to develop a dating app. Their body language was all wrong. Definitely not lovers. Or even wanna-be lovers. No romantic vibes from them at all.

Friends?

Their friendly demeanor with the waitress indicated locals.

The two women had their backs to her. The guy was directly in her field of vision.

He was gorgeous in that hot Latino way with an innate sensuality in his movements, but an unexpected guardedness surrounded him like a shroud. His dark brown hair, swept away from his face revealing cheekbones to die for and heavy-lashed dark brown eyes, brushed the back of his neck. Even in jeans and a short-sleeved Henley shirt, he looked like he belonged on the set of a romantic comedy or a movie with deep emotion and an everlasting love rather than in the rustic bar at the end of the world or, you know, the back of woods Vermont.

If she wasn't mistaken, he'd recently quit smoking. She recognized the signs. Every time the women spoke, he patted his pocket. Looking for a cigarette, she'd bet.

She was so caught up in her study she didn't even hear the waitress arrive.

"Hi, I'm Anne. What can I get you?"

"Oh!" Tracy skimmed over the menu again. "I'll take the pulled pork grilled cheese, but without the bread. Oh, and does that cherry barbeque sauce have flour in it? I know typically they don't, but can you check? And if it does then just leave it off."

The waitress scribbled furiously on one of those little order pads that flipped pages. Tracy hadn't seen an order pad like that in years. Except when she went to the diner in Cambridge with her business pals, the Billionaire Breakfast Club.

"Anything else?" She was practically rolling her eyes at Tracy.

She wasn't about to explain her dietary issues to the girl so she smiled tightly. "That'll do it." She handed the printed menu paper back to the girl.

Tracy could feel the server's frustration with her. Didn't people here have food allergies?

"Is that a Tiffany bracelet?" The waitress's eyes lit up, a turquoise glow close to the signature color of a Tiffany box and nearly the same color as the yin and yang charm on her platinum bracelet.

"Umm, yes."

"Oh. Em. Gee."

Not a common thing around here?

"I've only seen pictures on the internet," the waitress said wistfully. She reached out a finger as if to touch and then pulled it back. "Oops sorry!"

"It's all good." One thing Tracy had gotten used to was strangers touching her. She'd been doing campaign appearances and other media junkets with her family for years. It was amazing how being in the public sphere seemed to embolden people to do things they would never do with an anonymous stranger.

"I'm in love with high fashion. I'm a fashion design major at Moo U." Then she laughed.

Moo U?

Tracy's confusion must have been obvious. The fact that she wasn't able to conceal her thoughts meant she was far more tired than she thought. She'd been trained since preschool to always have a pleasant expression on her face and never let her true feelings show.

"Local university in Burlington," the waitress said.

"Ah." Tracy had to wonder what kind of fashion jobs were in very farm-centric, sparsely populated, rural Vermont.

The waitress seemed to read her mind again. "Right? I'll probably just come back here and work. Maybe I'll convince the Speakeasy owners to spruce up the waitstaff outfits." She gestured to her jeans and black T-shirt with *Speakeasy* across the chest. "Let me get your order in to the kitchen."

She watched another waitress deliver plates to a couple a few tables over. The food looked appetizing and the smells coming from the kitchen were heavenly.

Tracy smiled again and then tuned out the hot, angry guy and went online to read the news. Her stomach cramped at the negative headlines.

Young political candidate blasted by former fiancée, she cites dating app for presenting false information. Heiress bilks singles with elitist dating app. Up and coming politician deemed liar by ex-fiancée.

The verbiage got more and more vitriolic as she scrolled down the list. She was so intent on the articles that she barely noted as the waitress brought her non-sandwich and then walked away.

But as soon as Tracy looked at the plate, she realized there was an issue.

She raised her hand to get the girl's attention. Tracy waved her down and smiled brilliantly. "I need to send this back."

"Oh, did I mess up?"

Tracy said firmly, "I requested no bread."

The guy at the table behind her snorted.

"Oh, right. You told me that. I'm so sorry. I'll be right back."

Tracy's stomach growled as she handed her plate back to the waitress. Fortunately the place wasn't too busy. "You know, you should consider putting your Twitter and Instagram and Facebook social media handles on the menu. Or a QR code so people can easily access your profiles."

The girl blinked at her. "Uh, sure."

"So customers can document their time here. Share how fabulous the place is. It's free advertising from your customers."

"Thanks for the tip."

Tracy kept the smile on her face. She was a Thayer, after all. But she wasn't used to people ignoring her advice. Just in case, she repeated the no bread and no flour in the sauce request.

The hot guy glared at her as she repeated the modification on her order. What the heck crawled up his butt?

"I'll get this fixed right away," the waitress said.

"Thanks so much."

The waitress scurried away, and Tracy caught his gaze again.

Did he look familiar?

Shit. She couldn't afford to be recognized here. Based on the articles she'd been reading, the press was definitely looking for her. *"Tracy Thayer, apparent designer of the app and default princess of the political family, could not be reached for comment. Multiple messages left for her were not returned."*

Tracy chanced one more look at him. And he commented snidely, "Maybe you should just head to the kitchen and make your own."

The comment was not at all what she expected. The relief that rolled through her expelled in a laugh. She had no idea how to cook. She could scramble eggs and make sandwiches and cook burgers and toss a salad. But that was it. She ate out most of the time.

"I'd be in there all day. And nothing would taste as good as what the chef makes."

He blinked as if her good humor had taken him aback. Likely he was expecting a different response. But dealing with animosity was Customer Service 101. She could be friendly and agreeable in her sleep.

He nodded. "Enjoy your lunch. The chef here is fantastic."

"Aww, thanks, Colt," one of the women at the table said. "That's high praise coming from you."

So apparently his grumpiness didn't extend to his friends. Just to strangers one table over. She wasn't quite sure why he felt the need to be such a curmudgeon. Or why her order apparently offended him, but she shrugged off the weird hurt.

And resisted the urge to stick out her tongue at him.

After all, she had bigger problems than some random hot guy being annoyed with her. Besides, she'd never see him again.

When the waitress brought the sandwich filling back, without the bread, she asked Tracy, "Are you from Colebury?"

"No, just visiting."

"Huh, you look familiar."

Good thing she was just passing through. Otherwise, she'd need a disguise.

3

TRACY

A sudden swell of exhaustion rolled over her.

The adrenaline let down hit hard. She'd been running on fumes and anxiety for most of the day. She settled up her bill with the waitress and yawned. "Is there a hotel close by?"

She doubted there was a Four Seasons nearby, but maybe a Hilton or Hyatt. She could book a suite and take a nice long soak in a jacuzzi tub.

"The Three Bears Motor Lodge is just down the road."

Motor Lodge? Tracy tried to keep a smiling countenance but apparently she didn't quite conceal her grimace.

"Probably not up to your standards, Princess," hot guy interrupted in a biting tone.

Great. Now the hot guy was calling her princess. And the *move along* was implied.

All she wanted to do was get online and figure out what the hell happened with her app. But she had to be careful about disguising her identity. "Anything is fine," she said firmly.

The waitress wandered away.

"There're plenty of chain hotels in Burlington." His dismissive attitude rankled.

She smiled as sweetly as she could. "And how far away is that?"

"About forty-five minutes."

Her exhaustion was suddenly overwhelming. There was no way she could drive nearly an hour. "Can you tell me where to find the motor lodge?"

He raised a brow at her.

She fought the urge to snap at him.

"Follow the road and it will be on your right."

"Thank you," she said politely in her most haughty voice, projecting that political calm that had carried her through some of the most painful episodes of her life.

She'd literally trained her whole life to be as likable as possible. But right now, she wanted with an unexpected fierceness to clap back at him. It was completely irrational. She pushed the feeling aside. Thayers were always polite. Always. Everyone was a potential constituent or donor.

As she skimmed her gaze over his worn jeans and tight Henley, she doubted he was a donor, but appearances could be deceiving.

Again she thought that something about him looked familiar. Where did she know him from? She tilted her head and studied him objectively. Or tried to. He was seriously gorgeous and the scruff (a total no-no in her world) was incredibly weirdly appealing. The dark hair dusting the lower half of his face accented his mouth, which was surprisingly lush for a man.

"Memorizing details for a lineup?"

She jolted. She'd been unaccountably rude, but she wasn't about to apologize. She didn't feel the need to be nice. No one here knew her. That innate politeness and charm that she'd exuded her entire life had deserted her. "How long has it been since you quit smoking?"

He jerked back, and his eyes, a gorgeous dappled brown, widened. "A year," he muttered.

"It never gets easier."

"*You* used to smoke?"

No. But she'd coached her dad through quitting at least three times. And he had told her that every day he wished for a cigarette. "Family experience."

At that his gaze softened. "Family is everything."

"Yes, it is."

She'd spent her adult life protecting her family. Which was why she needed to stay hidden and concentrate on what went wrong with the app and how she'd been outed. She'd really like to speak to her dad or her brother to get an update.

Time for her to go. She'd stay at the motor lodge tonight and then move to Burlington tomorrow.

"You know I have this friend who makes…" She paused, checked herself. "Who recommends that you try this product." She rattled off Duke's cravings remedy. "He is convinced that if you substitute your habit with something else it will help you avoid the things that challenge your addictions."

He grimaced, as if the words were pulled from him with agonizing slowness, and said, "Thanks for the advice."

COLT

Humidity smothered the air like a physical presence looming in the background. His thoughts were particularly heavy as Colt returned to the tiny cabin he called home these days.

The encounter with the wealthy woman had left him dissatisfied and unsettled. Or maybe that was the conversation with Audrey and Phoebe. Or maybe it was that moment when he'd almost ordered a drink.

He pulled a hoe from the ramshackle shed next to the one-room cabin. The cabin wasn't much larger than the shed but the small, isolated space had been his refuge over the past year. He headed to the garden plot that he'd planted out of sheer boredom in the spring. Tending to the small strip of land had brought him an unexpected peace. The cardinals and blue jays and squirrels, little buggers, had been stealing his cherry tomatoes.

He'd picked up some netting at the tractor supply store to protect the fruit from the woodland animals trying to eat all his produce. He grabbed the netting and slung it over the tall plants, cursing as the black net tangled in the leaves. He wondered how much good it would actually do.

The rows of fall squash were coming along. His tomato plants were six feet tall. He'd begun to harvest the cucumbers and zucchini. He'd have to see if Phoebe wanted his zuchs, maybe to use in a daily special, otherwise they were going to go bad. Or maybe he could donate them to the local food bank. The squash reminded him of his signature vegetarian dish of roasted squash with sun-dried tomatoes, sliced cherry tomatoes, house-made burrata, and a hearty pesto.

He'd been particularly proud of his inventive vegetable sides, learning early from his mother the value of veggies with every meal.

Colt took stock of the rest of the rows of produce. The bunnies from the woods were ravaging his peppers.

He hadn't really thought through having a garden. Now he had all this produce and nothing to do with it. The nasturtium flowers, happy droopy blooms in yellow and orange, had kept away the cabbage worms and he had an explosion of zucchini.

He plucked some basil and inhaled the anise-like scent, bringing back memories of his zucchini fritters with a pesto aioli. His stomach rumbled.

Growing up in Connecticut his mother had a garden. The mouth-watering scent of fresh tomatoes, onions, spicy peppers, and coriander filling the air when she canned her *Molho à Campanha*, homemade salsa, was still a seminal childhood memory. His first memories of cooking were olfactory. Food was a sensory experience. Smell, taste, and touch were all important, but the first sense used to experience the food was the sense of smell.

He had all the ingredients to make her recipe. Tomatoes, peppers, coriander, vinegar, and oil.

But he didn't have a stockpot to skin the tomatoes. Which was exactly the way he wanted it.

He refused to be sorry and acknowledged the irony of being a master chef without a pot.

Colt propped the hoe against the shed, leaving the basket of vegetables on the miniscule porch so they didn't mock him with their presence in his kitchen, and went inside the cabin. He wasn't about to start cooking again.

No matter who asked him.

Cooking and addiction and bad behavior and fame were inextricably tied up in each other. He knew it was illogical, but he feared that if he went in the kitchen again, if he began seeking out fame again, he would fall back into old patterns.

How many times today had he reached for his pack of cigarettes?

Too many to count.

That brought him full circle to the woman at the Speakeasy. And whatever she'd been doing in Colebury.

He'd been unexpectedly attracted to her trim curves and smiling face. His body had stirred with an interest in sex that he hadn't had in over a year. The rich girl shouldn't have even tripped his libido. But she had popped into his mind often over the past few hours.

He forced the memory of her unexpectedly cheery countenance and light trilling laugh from his mind. After all, he'd never see her again.

TRACY

Tracy rolled over and peered at the bedside clock blearily.

It was eight a.m. She had trouble sleeping last night. Something—a pack of wild dogs?— had been howling in the middle of the night. The sharp yips had been terrifying.

She'd called the front desk because it sounded like someone was being murdered.

"That's coyotes." Mrs. Beasley, the owner, had laughed and hung up on her.

Coyotes?

They sounded horrible. And scary. And ravenous. And Tracy wasn't sure she wanted to leave the motel.

She got ready for her day and packed up so she could head into Burlington and find a larger chain hotel, preferably one with a restaurant attached and maybe a spa.

She stopped in the office. "Um, Mrs. Beasley?"

The old woman pretended she didn't hear Tracy. Except she knew she had. Because she spied on her every time she came or went from the little one-room cabin with décor leftover from the 1950s, to put her bags in her rental. Tracy was moving super slow because she was really dragging from stress and lack of sleep.

"Coffee?" she nearly whimpered.

"Machine in your room."

But it was weak, inexpensive coffee. Even if she brewed the entire packet for one cup it wouldn't be strong enough.

Tracy smiled with determination and said sweetly, "I like really strong coffee."

"The Busy Bean is the closest."

So she was going to have to drag her tired butt to a coffee shop. She couldn't wait to get to civilization. "I don't suppose you have a workout center?" Usually she started her day with a run on the treadmill or a Zumba class.

"Around here we just take a walk," Mrs. Beasley said.

Take a walk. "Outside?"

"Where else would we walk? The river is nice this time of year."

No treadmill apparently. Tracy kept her mouth shut and smiled politely. She wouldn't be here long.

There was a little toaster oven in the tiny kitchenette in her room. But she had no ingredients and no cooking ability. Tracy hadn't eaten since lunch yesterday. "Food?"

The answers were no, no, and no.

No room service. No Uber Eats this far out in the country. No delivery, except maybe the pizza place but they didn't do breakfast. Sob.

This morning had been a rude awakening. Thank goodness she wouldn't need to adjust to life in the country. This little town and the motor lodge were just a blip on her travel itinerary.

After checking out of the Three Bears, she headed to the Busy Bean, praying their coffee was stronger than the institutional stuff in her motel room.

The little bell over the door jingled as she entered. The line moved slowly and she took in the antique mismatched tables and upholstered chairs in dark colors and animal prints. The jam-packed shop emitted a comfortable yet wacky vibe. It smelled heavenly but Tracy figured that there wasn't much in the way of gluten free. She checked the specials board and the regular menu. Fortunately they had an option because the glass display case was filled mostly with cookies and pastries.

No one in the charming little storefront paid any attention to her and she got her breakfast to go.

Tracy couldn't wait to leave this town in her rearview mirror.

She planned to head to Burlington to purchase a printer and paper—sometimes you just had to go old school—so she could work on the question of how Esme had discovered her secret. Tracy also had to wonder if Esme had somehow tricked the system into matching her with Thomas.

When they'd been developing the software for the app, Britt had warned her that people would try to game the system to connect with the rich and famous. She had a high-end clientele. The cost to register for the app priced out less financially stable applicants but wasn't so expensive that regular people couldn't register. At least that's what she'd thought. But some of the headlines had been brutal.

The reason her app cost so much was because they ran extensive background checks and had excellent customer service. The counselors were trained to spot nuances and finesse the responses that the software spit out to give clients the best matches possible.

Esme would also have had to pass the background check and her client interview.

Tracy made a note to have Yolanda check into Esme and Thomas's match counselor as she drank her coffee on the way to Burlington.

She headed into the office supply store, ready to get her equipment and get to work.

She had a debit card under an alias. Growing up in a famous family meant she was well versed in the art of concealing her whereabouts for a quick weekend away.

She always had a bag packed with a thousand dollars in cash and an anonymous debit card loaded with another few thousand.

She strolled through the office supply store and grabbed a small portable printer, paper, an extra black ink cartridge and, just in case, another burner phone.

"Your card is out of money," the clerk said.

"What? That can't be correct." She smiled at the girl.

"I'm sorry, ma'am. But there isn't enough on the card to pay for the printer."

Tracy smiled tightly and pulled cash out of her wallet. Apparently, she'd forgotten to reload the card after the last time she'd traveled incognito. "Here's the rest." She mentally calculated how much cash she had left. About eight hundred dollars. Good thing she would be back home in a day or two.

Between the cost of the equipment, the motel room and food, she'd be out of money by then.

Once she loaded everything into her rental car trunk, she used a hotel booking app to look for a new place to stay in Burlington. But there was some sort of festival going on and all the hotels were packed, plus the room rates were jacked up. She even checked near Burlington University, searching for any alternative.

She banged her head back against the headrest.

Besides the fact that the hotels were full, the festival had exhibitors from as far away as Boston. There were Massachusetts license plates all over the town. She couldn't assume that she wouldn't be spotted here.

Even as she thought it, she grimaced. She'd be far less visible in a small hamlet.

She dialed Mrs. Beasley. "Is my old cabin available?"

There was a long pause. "Yes."

"Great. I'll be back to check in in about an hour."

And so that was why she ended up back at the Three Bears Motor Lodge, which at least had decent internet. Tracy emptied her car again, set up the printer and connected it to her laptop and got to work. She had a VPN so that her IP address couldn't be tracked. A virtual private network hid your location, bounced signals, fake IP addresses, blah, blah, blah. Pete had explained it to her, but she really only listened to the part where using it made her location secret. That was all she cared about after an overzealous reporter had identified her location from hacking her laptop and tracked her down.

She needed to send Pete an encrypted email and see if he'd found anything since yesterday. She had gotten rid of the burner phone she'd used to call her dad's office, when she'd spoken to Ashley. She pulled out a new phone and texted her brother in code.

But he hadn't answered.

She tried him again. She wanted to go home.

They didn't talk like they used to but growing up it had been Tracy and Thomas against the world. At one time he'd been her best friend.

Thomas only texted back:

Thomas: *Don't contact me right now. My life is a circus. Why the hell did you recommend that crackpot app?*

She blew out a breath and her shoulders slumped. Her phone pinged again.

Thomas: *Sorry. Love you. Talk later? In the middle of the firestorm right now. Have you checked the news?*

Tracy: *Love you back. Trying to come up with something to help. Have my CEO on it.*

Thomas: *thumbs up emoji.*

She was in exile. Cut off from her family and her friends. Over a scandal not completely of her making. Then she thought maybe Thomas was giving her a hard time. Maybe everything had died down and she could go home. She wouldn't know since she'd left her personal cell phone at her condo. Bernie could be trying to reach her right now to tell her it had all blown over and to come on back to Boston where she was comfortable and reasonably happy.

But when Tracy checked the news, the story was still making waves. So she got down to work trying to figure out how Esme had gotten her information, and trying to come up with a way to make this blow over so she could go back to her life.

4

TRACY

Three days later, Tracy was still at the Three Bears Motor Lodge.

She had been getting takeout and pouring over the information sent from Pete. They had been unable to find any indication that Esme had hacked confidential documents to discover her identity as the owner of Fairy Tale Beginnings.

And as a follow on, she'd begun looking at Esme and Thomas's match. As much as she didn't care for Esme, the program had matched her with Tracy's brother. When she looked at the data, their match made sense.

Yolanda had been dealing with the media fallout and resultant focus on the business. The publicity had increased their sales and applications were up. Tracy had crafted a statement for her employees, thanking them for their hard work and assuring them that nothing about their day to day would change.

But now she was going stir crazy. She'd been mostly locked in this little cabin motel room. She'd tried multiple times to get in touch with Bernie, with her dad, with her brother, and no one was calling her back.

Unfortunately it had been a really slow news week and the press was digging in on her and the app. They'd accused her of being elitist and trying to create a master race because of the cost of her program. When she'd set it up, she'd thought the buy-in fee of ten thousand dollars a year was a good figure. Not small change but also not exorbitantly expensive. But they were making it sound like she was stripping people of their life savings to find a good match.

She'd been in contact with her CEO about damage control. They'd done several press releases over the past two days, announcing that their background checks were strict and defending the buy-in cost.

They still had some people demanding refunds. And the fame seekers had gone on talk shows detailing horror dates, which anyone who'd ever been on a date through an app knew was bound to happen, even with all the safeguards she had put in place.

On the other side, she had a file full of testimonials from satisfied customers. But the loud and squeaky complainers got more coverage. Unhappy customers sold airtime, not happy couples.

She had people coming out of the woodwork to do interviews about her. They'd dredged up the article that D'Andre's girlfriend, Elise, had done last year about her friends, the Billionaire Breakfast Club.

And she was getting crap about that too.

#boycottfairytalebeginnings #boycottfairytale #elitistapp was trending on Twitter. The company's Facebook page had been spammed by trolls writing horrible things about her.

It honestly threw her off. People lied about things all the time. She knew that better than most. It was the reason she'd started the app in the first place. To give people a high level of comfort and confidence about their prospective partner.

They had done their best to eliminate undesirable people who misrepresented themselves. They did extensive background checks, credit analyses, and social media audits to make sure that the person was credible and to weed out people who were married or in a relationship or looking to swindle money from unsuspecting clients. They wanted clients who were serious about monogamy and finding a life partner. But nothing was foolproof.

People were angry and most of that rage was directed at Tracy. Even if the company shut down tomorrow, which she had no intention of doing, she would be fine.

The company was hers. She had a fierce sense of pride for what she'd built. And Esmerelda was not going to take that away from her. Dammit.

Tracy headed back over to the Speakeasy for lunch.

Her brain hurt.

It had been a long three days and she was ready to get back home.

She sat on a stool at the bar so she could order a glass of white wine and enjoy her lunch. Or at least try. She chose the last stool on the left and slid onto the seat.

A gust of cool air rushed over her. She looked up, thinking she must be sitting under an air conditioning vent but there wasn't one nearby.

"Oh, you probably don't want to sit there," said the manager, who according to the nametag was named Phoebe. "That's Hamish's seat."

Tracy shrugged and moved down one, curiosity getting the better of her since she hadn't seen anyone nearby. "Who's Hamish?"

"Our ghost."

She nearly spit out her chardonnay. "Excuse me?"

"I know. I felt the same way when they told me that the ghost of the artist who used to own this building was here, but there's no denying that Hamish is hanging around."

Tracy eyed the stool. A ghost? "I'll just go sit over there." She waved to the other side of the restaurant. "Bye, Hamish."

Tracy sat at the high-top table she'd occupied the first time she'd come here.

Phoebe swung by. "The usual?"

"That works."

Phoebe hustled toward the kitchen and Tracy pulled out the extra burner cell and dialed her brother. She was tired of waiting for someone to get back to her.

He answered on the first ring. "Who is this?"

"Hello, Thomas."

"What are you doing? We shouldn't have any contact right now. I'm trying to salvage my campaign."

That hurt but she let the rejection roll off. She was going stir crazy in Colebury. "Let me come help."

"No! I need you to stay out of the media. Stay hidden and don't get caught. How did you leave town? Please tell me you didn't take your Tesla."

Her electric car was an understated white. And while there were definitely more electric cars in the Northeast than a few years ago, the Tesla would stand out in the wilds of Vermont.

"I rented a car."

"Under your own name?"

Jeez, he was treating her like an idiot. No wonder Esme had left him.

"I had a friend do it."

Even if she'd done it herself, she would have used an alias. She liked to travel a lot. And the press was unnervingly interested in her life even though she wasn't the politician. Maybe because of that article last year about her friends, the BBC. But she'd put together a pile of aliases over the last few years. In the past that had worked just fine.

"Great. Don't tell me what it is."

"I'm in—"

"No. I don't want to know."

"But I want to help."

"Trust me, we need you out of the picture so you can't do any more damage."

That hurt. But she still wanted to help.

"I can—"

"Seriously, stay away and stay hidden. We're in major damage control mode. Esme is threatening to tell the media about you-know-what unless I give her money."

That bitch.

And of course, that right there was why she was never honest with her boyfriends. And if she wasn't honest, how could she ever find a partner? Intimacy was difficult when one partner was holding back. She'd never been able to trust anyone enough to share their family secrets.

Speaking of money. If he wanted her to stay away, she was going to need more. "Listen, I need some cash. Can you wire me money?"

"Figure it out, Trace. I don't have time to deal with your petty issues."

She'd hardly call not having money a petty issue.

"Don't use your credit cards, don't use your cell phone. Just stay off the radar until we can get a handle on this fiasco."

"But—"

"And you need to shut down that matchmaking app before it causes any more trouble."

What?

Fairy Tale Beginnings was her business. She wasn't about to shut it down. It was her baby. The one business idea she'd conceived of and implemented on her own. She'd used the skills of New Wins Tech to set it up, but the app was all her. Giving people their fairytale and happily ever after was her dream, embedded in her psyche ever since she was thirteen. Getting rid of the app would be like cutting off her arm. The lump in her throat had grown to the size of an overly large bridal bouquet. But she couldn't get out the refusal fast enough.

"I am not shutting it down." Her company wasn't just her. She had employees and other businesses that relied on her business doing well.

"Don't call again." Thomas was brutal. "Don't come home until the media furor has died down." Then he abruptly hung up.

He hung. Up. On her.

She frowned at the phone in her hand.

She wasn't about to shut down her app. She'd matched plenty of couples with no problems. The reality was that the app wasn't one hundred percent effective. Nothing could be. But she had a high success rate. As a matter of fact, there were entire Instagram pages devoted to Fairy Tale Engagements and Fairy Tale Weddings portraying couples who were engaged or married because of meeting on her app.

She'd done that. Helped them find their fairy tale. Her!

Hopefully this whole thing would blow over in a day or two. A freak summer snowstorm, or a shakeup at the Red Sox, or some other political scandal would come along and dominate the next news cycle. Right?

Phoebe placed her plate of a pile of pulled pork, gouda cheese and cherry BBQ sauce on a bed of lettuce on the wood tabletop. "Trouble?"

Her entire life had gone sideways.

"Minor inconvenience." Groomed in the art of distraction at an early age, Tracy gushed about the food. "This looks delicious. As always."

Phoebe put the check on the table. "Whenever you have a chance."

The bite of delicious food soured in her stomach. She was running out of money.

Anne, her waitress from the first day she was here, rushed into the dining room, buzzing by Tracy and heading for Phoebe. "Sorry I'm late. My professor kept us after again. Is there time to grab a plate before I start?"

Phoebe glanced around. "Make it quick."

Anne sat at the bar and wolfed down a fancy-looking slider.

Then bussed her plate and came to collect Tracy's payment and tip.

Tracy carefully counted out her money. Thought about the cost of the motel room and the cost of food.

This shit needed to wrap up soon. She was running out of cash.

"What did you eat?" Tracy asked curiously. She'd been in a rut, ordering the same thing every day. Maybe it was time to try something new.

"The special." The waitress counted out her change. "We get to eat for free. It's one of the perks of working here. Plus they pay pretty well."

An idea sparked as she considered her dwindling pile of money. After all, she ate out all the time. She could handle waitressing. Right? *I mean, how hard could it be?*

When Phoebe walked by, Tracy stopped her. "Excuse me."

"Problem?"

She was pretty sure the Help Wanted sign was still in the window. "Do you still need workers?"

Phoebe eyed her, her gaze skimming over Tracy's short-sleeved silk button-up shirt and cropped khaki trousers. "Are *you* asking?"

There was enough incredulity in her voice that Tracy bristled. "I am."

"Have you ever worked in a restaurant before?"

"No. But I eat out a lot." She gave her a brilliant smile.

Phoebe laughed. "The job is a little more complex than that."

Tracy said earnestly, "I am a fast learner, and I won't eat much." But not having to pay for all her meals would totally help out. If she was careful about money it could last her while she was in exile. She might feel a little guilty since she wasn't planning on staying long.

But once she was done, she'd never see these people again. And while she was here, she could help them out as well. After eating here for a few days, she knew that their customer traffic was uneven but the food was top-notch. They just needed a little marketing boost.

Phoebe eyed her. "What other experience do you have?"

"I'm excellent at marketing." She left off image consulting. That would bring up questions she didn't want to answer. And really, she didn't think they needed an image consultant or a spin doctor. "As a matter of fact, I've been suggesting to the waitstaff that you might want to put your social media handles on the menu. That way people can tag you when they tweet or post about their experience."

Phoebe shuddered as soon as Tracy mentioned social media.

Well, it was their loss if they didn't want to increase their visibility.

Phoebe shook her head skeptically. "I'm not sure you'd be happy here."

Her soft words were like a sharp knife to the heart.

Tracy Thayer wasn't used to begging for anything. She'd pretty much been handed life on a platter and she'd taken that all for granted. "Please," she asked. "I could use the money."

Phoebe sighed. "When can you start?"

"Right away," Tracy shot back.

Phoebe eyed her one more time. "Okay. Trial basis." She seemed to understand that Tracy had big problems and could sympathize with her predicament.

"Yes!" Tracy pumped her fist in the air.

"What's your name?" Phoebe asked.

Oops. She hadn't thought that far ahead. She shouldn't use the alias she'd been using with the debit card. Right? But then she remembered that she'd brought Cee-Cee. That last-minute impulse was paying off. Although if she burned through Cee-Cee, she potentially wouldn't be able to use her again.

"Cee-Cee." When she was little, after the shock that transformed her world, she'd created an imaginary persona. Cee-Cee was the girl she wished she was. She'd spent hours imagining

Cee-Cee's life. She'd even had a fake identification made. And Cee-Cee would totally work in a restaurant.

"You sure about that?" Phoebe raised an eyebrow, as if she could see through Tracy's lies.

Tracy channeled her imaginary identity. "My full name is Cecilia, but I prefer to be called Cee-Cee." That seemed to appease the questions that lingered in Phoebe's gaze.

"Can you start tonight?"

"Sure." Tracy fought the urge to wipe her damp hands on her khakis.

Phoebe sized her up. "Small for the T-shirt?"

A T-shirt. She hadn't worn a cotton T-shirt since sailing camp in sixth grade. "Yes."

"Okay. I'll give you a shot." Phoebe nodded as if she'd made up her mind. "Oh, wear jeans. And comfortable shoes."

Ugh.

Jeans? "Is there a clothing boutique close by? I need to buy a pair of jeans." She wondered if Lily Pulitzer had some cute ankle crop jeans she could pair with the quite unfashionable T-shirt.

Phoebe snorted. "A boutique?"

Tracy nodded. She didn't know what was so funny. They had to buy their clothes somewhere. If she wasn't mistaken, Phoebe's clothes could totally have come from a boutique in New York. Her pants and shoes were premium quality. The T-shirt couldn't be helped.

"Yes."

"Oh, honey. Welcome to the country. Try the tractor supply store."

Tractor supply?

What had she gotten herself into?

An hour later, Tracy arrived at the tractor supply store and pulled into the gravel and dirt parking lot. Outside the main building, around the side, were riding mowers, plow attachments and some giant V-shaped things.

Inside was an assortment of tools that she had no idea what

they were for. A giant scythe, hanging on hooks on a pin and hook wall, looked like it came from a horror film. Other giant tools were displayed in haphazard fashion. Tracy skirted the wall of large weapons and a line of shiny new lawn mowers in a straight row.

There was even a section for camping. She shuddered. Cook stoves and propane and sleeping bags. People were not meant to sleep on the ground.

Another section was filled with seed packets and small trowels and hand shears and had a sliding door that led outside to the gardening nursery section.

In the back of the giant warehouse, she found the clothing section. A wall of jeans and shorts folded in stacks, T-shirts, plaid shirts, and tank tops with odd sayings like "Farm-er (fahr-mer) *noun*. A person who is outstanding in their field," "I don't need therapy, I just need to drive my tractor," and "Never underestimate a woman who loves goats."

Goats?

Tracy looked at the sizes for the jeans and had no idea what to wear. She was flummoxed.

COLT

Colt came into the tractor supply store to pick up some new gardening gloves. He'd torn a hole in his old pair yesterday.

He never expected to see the woman from the Speakeasy again. She'd unexpectedly invaded his dreams the past few nights. He'd awoken aroused and annoyed.

Kind of an amazing combination.

She smelled really good. Like a mix of roses and patchouli. He inhaled her scent and then cursed himself. Her skin was the color of the blush roses that had been a hallmark of his eponymous restaurant in Boston. The roses, his mother's favorites, had been

on every table in the small dining room and on the maître d'
stand.

He should walk the other way. Head to the garden section and
forget about her. But he was inexplicably drawn to her. "You look
confused."

She jolted. She'd been so busy staring at the wall she didn't
hear him approach. "Oh!"

"What's the problem?"

"I typically wear European sizes."

He sighed. "Of course you do."

"What does that mean?"

This woman was the epitome of wealthy and entitled.
European sizes for fuck's sake. "Why are you buying clothes at
the tractor store?" She was about the same size as his sister
Maria. He reached out and grabbed the same waist size his sister
wore. He held out the jeans and she gasped at the scars on his
hands. Years in the kitchen had left him with scars and burn
marks. Most of the time he forgot he had them. A hazard of
his job.

His former job.

"Oh my gosh, what happened?"

Up close he could get lost in the cornflower of her eyes. The
shards of darker blue in a starburst reminded him of a kaleido-
scope and he found himself wanting to edge closer. She'd
forgotten to put on that polished, insincere demeanor and the
difference felt striking. Like he was seeing into her like no one else
ever had.

That didn't mean he wanted her seeing into him. "That size
should work."

She took the hint and let her question drop. "I appreciate your
help."

He couldn't stop himself from asking again. She triggered
something in him. A curiosity that had been missing for a while.
He'd been subsisting on a bland diet of self-reflection and recrimi-
nation for months. "Why are you here?"

"I'm going to work at the Speakeasy," perky and peppy, she chirped.

What? He couldn't help it. The unexpected mirth started in his belly and spread through his body, his diaphragm contracting as he laughed in great big loud guffaws.

"I don't see what's so amusing," she said haughtily.

He wiped away the tears that had streamed over his cheeks. "Have you ever worked a day in your life?"

"Of course. I've been working since I was fifteen."

He'd bet his Iron Chef trophy that she'd never toiled in a restaurant. "In a bar?" The Speakeasy was more than a bar but the distinction likely was lost on Little Miss European sizes.

"Of course not. But there's a first time for everything." She smiled sunnily, her optimism blinding.

He glanced at the ballet flats on her feet. "You need shoes."

But his traitorous brain went to other more personal things. If she wore heels, she'd be just the right size to kiss. They would fit together like chateaubriand in a puff pastry, a classic French combination.

"These shoes are amazingly comfortable." She defended her footwear choice hotly. "They are butter-soft Italian leather. I got them in Venice last year."

"They have thin soles and no support. Your feet will be killing you in a few hours."

"How can you be so sure?"

He remembered his first time working in a restaurant. Even at fifteen—yeah, he'd been the same age as the debutante when he started working—after a ten-hour day bussing tables, his feet had been killing him.

"Experience." One that he had no desire to relive.

He remembered the excitement of his first day. He'd decided on his career choice at a young age. That visceral memory of helping his dad season a piece of meat and the sizzle when it hit the grill, and the sense of accomplishment and pride that he'd felt when his family was fed. Somewhere along the way he'd lost that simple pleasure and inspiration, caught up in awards and perfection and chasing the next accolade. Instead of celebrating simple pleasures, he'd become mired in the race, self-medicating with cigarettes and scotch in a never-ending chain of stimulants and depressants.

"Hey, are you okay?" She placed her fingers on his forearm.

The touch zapped him back to reality. And the memory of those hot, sweaty dreams returned with a vengeance.

She realized she was touching him at the same time he did and snatched her hand away.

"Never better," he lied.

She studied him like a department of health inspector searching for evidence of rodents.

"I'm sure these—" she twisted her foot to look at the completely inadequate shoes "—will be fine."

Her ankle was delicate, her feet tiny, everything about her screamed feminine and…sugar sweet.

"They're your aching feet." He shrugged. "Your choice, Deb."

She jolted. "My name isn't Deb. It's T…Cee-Cee."

That weird hitch in her voice made him pause. Then he realized whatever her issues were, they were none of his business. He didn't want them to be his business.

"Whelp, Cee-Cee, good luck." He forced himself to turn away and head for the gardening supply section. He muttered as he walked away, "You're going to need it."

"Before you go…" She stopped him.

"What now?"

"Since you're here, can you tell me where I could find a dry cleaner?"

He laughed again.

"Launderette?"

"The kind where you drop off your clothes and they wash them for you?"

"Exactly," she said in triumph.

"Boston."

Her face fell.

"There's a laundromat on the corner of Elm and Second. Although I'm pretty sure the motor lodge has coin-operated machines in the main building."

Her blue eyes widened in shock.

"Yes. You're going to have to do your own."

He was still laughing about the look on her face hours later.

5

COLT

Colt couldn't get the wealthy girl out of his mind.

He wondered how she was faring. The memory of her face when he'd told her she'd have to do her own laundry brought a chuckle. He couldn't remember the last time he'd laughed that hard. Before he knew it, he was in his old truck—he'd sold the fancy Mercedes he'd bought as a symbol of success—and on his way to the Speakeasy.

He'd been gardening and come up with an idea for a vegetarian main course. Maybe he'd run it by Phoebe, see if she was interested in his thoughts, and then head home.

He parked near the employee entrance. That was not an admission that he was going to become an employee and cater events at the Speakeasy. He went through the customer entrance. They'd done a nice job with the décor. He knew from developing his own restaurants that every small detail contributed to the ambiance of a venue.

However after the incident, he'd become persona non grata in the restauranteur world. He'd sold his restaurants, and the new owner had promptly changed the name. Which was smart.

Hard to have a high-end exclusive business and appeal to the right clientele when your head chef was labeled a lunatic and unstable. Even successful restaurants operated on thin margins. One bad month could torpedo a booming business. Even if he'd wanted to keep cooking and maintain his restaurants, he would have likely had to close in a few months.

So he'd sold the restaurants and equipment and left that world behind.

Colt sauntered into the Speakeasy's open seating area and took in the chaos.

Phoebe paused, carrying a plate of sliders. They must be really busy if she was also serving customers. "Did you change your mind?" The hope in her voice was hard to take.

"Just came in for a quick bite."

"Got to see you twice in one week." Phoebe waved toward the bar seating. "Have a seat at the bar."

The unusual-shaped, almost oval bar dominated the main dining room space, sitting in the center like the main course platter at a Sunday buffet.

He wanted to object. Sitting that close to temptation was not what he'd anticipated but as he glanced around the packed restaurant, he knew he couldn't in good conscience take up even a two-top. They were too busy. "Good crowd."

Colt slid onto a seat at the bar. Nodded to the empty stool next to him. "Hey, Hamish." The idea of a ghost tickled his sense of humor, but the rush of cool air was a bit of a surprise.

Ty, the bar manager, gave him a chin lift. "What can I get you?"

Colt stared at the bottles displayed on the glass shelving, highlighted by the antique lamps hanging from the ceiling, his gaze automatically zooming in on his choice of poison, the bottle of Lagavulin. His mouth watered at the anticipation of feeding the beast inside him.

He could almost feel the burn from the 80 proof alcohol

content and the heat as the elixir slid down his throat. Instead, he burned with shame. "Club soda with a lemon."

Ty quickly filled his order and slid the drink in front of him. "Lemme know if you need anything else."

The television was on mute while the Red Sox destroyed the Yankees. A couple of other single guys hunched over plates of fries and drank beer with their gazes glued to the game. Personally, Colt preferred hockey but the Bruins preseason hadn't started yet.

Phoebe dropped off the sliders giving an intimate smile to Sam Tremblay, a local guy who'd been gone for awhile but had returned home to help out his grandmother and aunt with Crystal Persuasion, their new age-y shop with metaphysical stuff like energy healing and tarot card readings. Even Colt could tell the two had something going on. Good for her.

Colt quickly rattled off an order for Breakfast for Dinner—a sweet potato hash and poached eggs with a maple siracha drizzle that reminded him of a hash he used to make, although the siracha drizzle was a nice touch—and then swiveled around to watch the controlled chaos on the restaurant floor rather than stare at the tower of booze.

His gaze found her immediately. Her normally perfectly styled hair hung in limp wisps against her cheeks. She held her paper and pencil at the ready but her white-knuckled grip on the pencil belied her smile. Tension tightened the corners of her glass-blue eyes and her mouth was seconds from tipping down.

She was waiting on the table behind him.

"What can I get you?" The deb was back. She was trying to pull up her sunny persona but all that forced good cheer was starting to crack around the edges. Yet somehow she managed to make the jeans and T-shirt look feminine and high-class.

The family of four started ordering. Every single dish had some modification, and he wondered how she felt about changes to the menu now. The stray thought amused him.

She repeated their order back to them, getting about half the modifications incorrect. But she managed to charm them out of annoyance and before she left they were actually giving her tips on how to remember their order. Instead of being aggravated, they were all smiles.

He listened absently as he studied the rest of the room. He missed the frenetic camaraderie of restaurant life. Of course at the end he'd been a tyrant rather than one of the group. Even he couldn't stand his own company.

"Yo, Cee-Cee," Ty called to her as she was about to walk away. "One order of Breakfast for Dinner."

She grabbed the ticket from the bartender and turned to go back to the kitchen, jolting to a halt at the sight of Colt.

"Come to gloat?" Her normally peppy voice had an exhausted lilt to it.

He had been thinking along those lines, but he was disoriented by how much he hated seeing her defeated. The angry asshole in him wanted to rub it in, deliver a heartfelt *I told you so*, but he restrained the impulse.

"How are the feet?" He wasn't sure but he thought he'd detected a slight limp.

"Absolutely fabulous." She was lying through her orthodontia-ed white teeth.

"Soak them in Epsom salts tonight after you get off."

Except the motor lodge didn't have a bathtub, just a small shower.

"Miss." An older woman raised her hand. "I asked for more water ten minutes ago."

"Oh good golly. I'm so sorry," she called out. Her smile slipped. "Got to run."

Colt watched as she scurried away.

TRACY

Oh my God. Her feet were killing her.

Tracy wanted to collapse into a puddle of agony. She hadn't been on her feet this much since she'd done the Jimmy Fund Walk to raise money for cancer research in high school. She preferred her exercise in the water or on the tennis court.

How in the world did people do this for a living?

She was exhausted as she trudged toward the wait station to grab the pitcher of water.

"Hydration is so important!" she said in a sing-songy voice on the way to refill the woman's glass, for the millionth time, when another table flagged her down.

"We've been waiting for our check." The man glanced at his rugged watch impatiently. Their hiking backpacks on the floor next to their chairs.

"Oh gosh. I'm so sorry. I'll be right back with that. You all need to get on your way." Tracy wanted to make up for making them wait. "According to my other table, there's a gorgeous walking trail on the way out of town if you want to walk off those yummy turkey sliders." She smiled and they preened under her attention.

She managed to connect the two tables of hikers and by the time she'd come back with their check, the two couples were deep in conversation about local hiking trails.

Her humiliation was complete when the hot grumpy guy had walked in and sat at the bar. She was pretty sure he'd been a nanosecond from saying I told you so.

But she was too tired to slug him. Even though she never would. A Thayer was always pleasant even in the face of animosity. But her Thayer genes were dead on their feet and the newly awakened Cee-Cee wanted to go HAM on his smug face.

Her entire body ached. Her arms were sore from carrying trays of food even though she lifted weights regularly. Her trainer would be laughing his ass off at her.

She was going to give him a piece of her mind...once she was able to move again.

And her feet...were on fire.

Even the tops of her feet were sore. She didn't even know that was a thing.

She was only supposed to be bussing tables and learning the ropes today but they were super busy and under-staffed so she'd been thrown right in the deep end.

Tracy printed the hikers' receipt and tucked it in a folder. She dropped it on their table and walked by the family of four.

Shit. She'd forgotten to put their order in.

She rushed back to the kitchen. "I forgot this."

The chef looked at her with more than a little disgust.

"I'm so sorry." She felt compelled to defend herself. "It's my first day and I'm still getting the hang of how everything works."

The chef didn't comment. "Order twenty-four is up. Then take a break. I'll get someone else to deliver this when it's ready."

A break? That sounded like heaven.

She would never complain about writing a press release again. So many words to weigh. So many responses to anticipate, statements to craft and arguments to defend positions. But the mental intricacies were nothing compared to trying to remember ten different table's orders.

Tracy grabbed the order of sweet potato hash with the fried egg on top and then glanced at the check. Great.

She headed determinedly toward the bar. She dropped the ceramic plate on the wood slab, determined to be professional. "Is there anything else you need?"

Please say no. Please say no.

Her feet were screaming with the need to sit down.

"Well..." He stared at his plate.

She hadn't even taken the order. "Please tell me that your order is right. I didn't even take it. I couldn't have screwed that up!" She was a step removed from wailing.

He snickered. "Going that well, is it?"

She wasn't about to admit that she had thought this would be easy. "If you'll excuse me, I get to take a break now."

Where she could fall apart in peace.

And maybe consider quitting. She could just go back to Boston and cower in her condo until this all blew over. It was probably already a memory in the news cycle, and her father and brother were just punishing her for messing up their carefully crafted plans.

Because seriously, there had to be an easier way to make money. How in the world did people make a living doing this? Her tips had been so-so. But she couldn't blame her customers. She was terrible.

She knew it.

She had never complained to a restaurant owner or chef—the press would have a field day with privilege—but she'd mentally chastised them when they'd gotten her order wrong.

"Not as easy as it seems."

"I take back every bad word I ever thought about a server," she said tiredly.

"Good to know you can admit when you are wrong."

"I'd admit to killing a small animal right now if it gave me five extra minutes of break time." She was too exhausted to couch her exhaustion in polite terms.

"It gets easier."

She didn't think she'd be finding out. She was close to telling Phoebe she couldn't do this anymore. Forget the fact that she was down to her last hundred dollars and she only had two days left on her prepaid motel room.

She was going home.

Breaking news flashed across the bottom of the television screen. The past few days had been unbelievably nice. She'd been removed from the twenty-four-hour news cycle. Normally she'd be monitoring multiple channels for any topical news and making sure her father had an appropriate response ready, constantly preparing to spin his positions.

The respite from the high-intensity atmosphere of her job had been nice. She always thought she'd go crazy if she didn't have access to constant feedback. But she'd been surprisingly rested.

She wondered what was happening.

Then she saw her name. Her father's opponent was shouting to the rooftops that her app was barely a step up from pimping and that it violated her father's position on family values. Never mind that there were plenty of other dating apps with far racier premises and less focus on forming lasting relationships. He was demanding accountability from her. Her first instinct was to go defend her company and her vision. But she had to trust the process.

Shit. She couldn't leave now.

The new bartender, Demetrio, was pulling drinks but his gaze kept returning to the television. She needed to distract him. Stat.

She'd caught Anne checking out Demetrio multiple times. She had a Celtics keychain that Tracy had seen her put in her locker earlier. "Hey Demetrio, are you a sports fan?"

"Yep." He used the shaker to do a little dance as he samba'd his way behind the bar. He was dressed in the bar uniform but it looked anything but standard on his athletic body while he performed his sexy moves.

"Can I take some video of you?"

"Video?" He flushed with embarrassment. "Uh…"

"To post on social media."

"Sure. I guess."

"You'll be an immediate viral sensation." She smiled at him. "So what's your favorite team?"

He expertly poured the drink into a highball glass. "Celtics."

"Oh!" she exclaimed, totally fake. "How funny. Anne too."

"That wasn't at all subtle," grumpy hot guy said under his breath. She still didn't know his name, but she ignored him, finished the video, and set it to some Latin music. Then she realized she couldn't post on any of her existing accounts. As a member of her father's press and communications team, she had an official account, plus her own personal Instagram and a Fake Instagram. She had set up the Finsta since sometimes she just wanted to be silly. But a couple of her friends knew her Finsta account, so that was out as well.

She tapped her mouth, then shrugged. What the hell. She created a new profile, @ceeceeinthecountry and chuckled to herself as she uploaded the twenty-second video. Come for the drinks, stay for the entertainment. She tagged the Speakeasy and then wondered if the town of Colebury had an account. #countrylife #hotbartenders #ceeceeinthecountry #citygirlgoescountry #speakeasy #coleburyvt.

Grumpy guy stayed silent as she tried to maneuver the bartender into talking to the waitress.

"What are you doing?"

She jumped. She hadn't forgotten about him. She was trying desperately to ignore him. "Facilitating."

"Why do you care?"

She paused. "Because they seem like they'd make a good match."

"Why not let them discover that on their own?"

Tracy couldn't help herself. She was good at matchmaking. She knew she was. This current fiasco had shaken her confidence in herself and her abilities, but the only way to move forward was through. Sometimes people just needed a little nudge. She propped her hands on her hips and tilted her chin in the air. "I am a fairy godmother."

He snorted.

But she ignored him. For just a moment she wanted to do something she excelled at. Waiting tables had been humbling. Trying to keep track of multiple orders and the timing of food being released from the kitchen and just the sheer amount of walking threw her off balance. She'd spent her morning trying to figure out if and how her app had been breached and her late afternoon and evening running around the Speakeasy. She was exhausted and dispirited.

She was good at two things: matchmaking and marketing. She could check matchmaking off her list for today. And setting up a social media account as her alias Cee-Cee was fun.

She was hyperaware of him sitting next to her and felt the need to distract him. Her whole body ached. "I had no idea how hard this was."

He dug into his hash. Even the way he chewed was sexy. That had to be illegal. Right? And someone as irritating as him should not be sexy. Her body needed to get the message.

He stopped eating to look at her. "I'm sure." There was a note of censure in his tone. A disdain that she didn't understand.

She didn't know why he didn't like her.

Everyone liked her. She went out of her way to be cordial and welcoming. But this guy had a shield around him so thick that even in a crowded bar he sat alone and isolated. He watched the action on the restaurant floor with a bit of wistfulness. And she wondered what his story was.

"Is there a reason you don't like me?" She couldn't believe those words had spilled from her mouth. She had spent her entire life being nice, being polite, and being agreeable. But when she asked him, there had been a challenge in her voice. The freedom was liberating.

He ate his hash slowly as if savoring each bite. The food was pretty amazing.

She waited as he chewed. He glanced out the side of his eyes, a gorgeous deep brown that she totally should not have noticed. This close to him his scent was a mixture of sunscreen and warmth and clean sweat as if he'd spent the day in the sun. Earthy. Masculine. And very, very sexy.

She shouldn't notice how sexy he was. He didn't like her.

She was tired of waiting for an answer. She propped her hands on her hips and leaned into his personal space. "You don't even know me."

"I don't have to know you." He flipped a glance her way. "I know your type."

Her *type*? "What type? Nice? Invested in making people happy?"

"Rich, clueless, and arrogant."

"Yeah, well you're grumpy, irritating, and wrong."

Her feet throbbed and now her head ached. She rarely cried but everything about today had been difficult. Feeling like a fish out of water wasn't pleasant. She wanted to go back to her busy life and her active friendships. But she was stuck here for the moment. And her eyes burned.

Tracy took a deep breath and focused on something else. She needed to channel her alter ego. What would Cee-Cee do?

She had imagined Cee-Cee for so long. Cee-Cee spoke her mind and didn't worry about optics. She didn't even know what optics were.

"I'm making the best of a bad situation." She defended her actions.

But as she looked at him, she realized there was more going on than his slightly derogatory comments about her. He'd done a weird turn thing so he wasn't facing the bar but sort of sideways. It had to be hard to eat that way.

"You need to stop running away from your problems."

Her heart stopped. Did he know who she was? Hopefully he was just intuitive. "Easier said than done."

"Of course it is. Hard things aren't supposed to be easy." He said it as if he was intimately familiar with hard things.

She wasn't about to let him off the hook. He clearly had his own issues.

"Maybe you need to take your own advice," she shot back. Damn straight.

"Maybe you're right."

Ha.

6

TRACY

She was still thinking about the hot guy the next day. She'd almost asked him who he was. He looked so familiar. But no use in opening that box. Especially since she didn't want anyone taking too close a look at her.

Right now she was more worried about how she was going to pay for more nights at the hotel. She and Yolanda had gone over the data multiple times and she couldn't find any glitches or intrusions into the system that would have revealed her identity. Which meant somehow Esme had found the information another way.

They needed to investigate Esme but that wasn't something that Tracy could do. Yolanda had already called a private investigator. She needed opposition research on her brother's ex-fiancée. Stat.

While she hadn't cared for Esme, she had never considered having her investigated beyond the thorough background investigation they ran at Fairy Tale Beginnings. Doing that hadn't been on her radar. She'd been happy for her brother.

Thomas had not been as upset about the truth about their

parent's marriage. But when Tracy found out, she had been devasted. Her parents' fairy-tale romance, the story that the press bandied about as canon, was all a lie.

Her parents both had affairs. They just kept them very, very private.

She had bigger problems than her parent's fabrication of their romance and their lies to the public. In her quest to give romance and happily ever afters to normal people, someone had discovered her secret and sold the information or they'd breached her supposedly unbreachable software.

She'd worked on the data all day and couldn't find any answers. Then she'd come to the Speakeasy for her shift, although she pretty much expected to get fired. She really was a terrible waitress.

It was late. And her feet were killing her. Phoebe had asked if she could stay later; one of the other waitresses had a babysitting emergency and Tracy needed the money, so she'd agreed. She'd managed to get a pair of tennis shoes from the local shoe store but to buy shoes with enough support she'd had to spend money she didn't really have. She'd also had to buy more gas for the car—which seemed crazy since she was mostly just going back and forth between the motel and work. And another night's rent for the motor lodge was due.

To her surprise, sexy grumpy guy walked in about half an hour before the bar area was set to close. The kitchen had shut down thirty minutes ago, and the chefs had all gone home. Her job was to buss the rest of the plates and wipe down the tables and chairs with sanitizer.

It had been a quiet night and today's bartender, Matteo, was cleaning the bar while the last of the drinkers finished up their cider and ales.

Hot grumpy guy took one look at her and glared. She was sitting on the stool at the end of the bar taking a quick ten-minute break.

Tracy sighed and slipped her shoes back on. "Back to the

grind, Hamish." She'd taken to chatting with the ghost on her breaks.

Before she could get to him to tell him that the kitchen was closed, he pushed his way through the swinging door.

Tracy followed him into the kitchen to chastise him. "Hey, you aren't supposed to be in here. Kitchen is—" She stopped cold. He stood in the center of the restaurant kitchen on the rubber honeycomb floor mat with a lost look on his face. "—closed."

"I am aware."

Tracy frowned at him. "Then you should leave."

"I wish." He headed for the large walk-in refrigerator.

Holy shit. She just figured out how she knew him. Grumpy hot guy was Colton Vega. He was thinner and had a deeper tan than a few years ago. He had been the darling of the celebrity chef circuit until he had a breakdown. He had lost his shit and thrown something, burning his sous chef and destroying his career.

Tracy had eaten at Vega's a few years ago. His food was transcendent—which said a lot since she was more about food as fuel than as a culinary experience. She didn't think a lot about it. But that meal had been amazing. One of the top meals she'd ever eaten.

Colton Vega.

She was pretty sure her mouth was hanging open. Colton Vega. She couldn't wrap her mind around the fact that a Michelin-starred chef was chopping up vegetables in a kitchen in rural Vermont.

Celebrity blowups weren't a regular part of her news intake. Unless they referenced a dating app. Or took a political position. She remembered being sad about his demise and then she'd forgotten all about him.

But things were coming back to her. Rumors about late-night drinking and out-of-control behavior.

She followed him into the fridge. "You can't be in here."

"'Fraid I can, Deb."

"I told you, it's Cee-Cee." She straightened her spine.

"Well, Cee-Cee, I've got to get to work. So you can head out."

She couldn't leave him alone in here. Could she?

What if he had an episode and wrecked the kitchen? Technically she was responsible. Although really what were they thinking to put her in charge? She was a stranger. She could be a serial killer for all they knew. Or a thief. Or, or…something worse that she couldn't even think of right now.

When Phoebe had asked her to stay late, clearly she was last on the list of employees to handle things, but everyone else had plans, so Tracy agreed. Since she'd been entrusted with closing up, she needed to stick around. But she'd be sure to mention to Phoebe that she really shouldn't trust a stranger.

He headed for the giant sink and scrubbed with the antibacterial industrial cleaner using his fingers to clean between his other fingers and scrubbing up his arms to his elbows. Then he flipped a towel from the stack of clean linens on the corner of the counter and dried off his arms.

His very sexy arms. Focus, Tracy!

"Can I…help with anything?"

He turned around and glared at her. "Are you still here?"

Sweat had formed on his brow and he had a slightly panicked look in his eyes.

"Here and ready to assist." She wasn't about to leave. Hopefully she wouldn't have to be more assertive. She executed a mock salute.

"You know how to cook?"

She laughed nervously, because of course she didn't. "I am a great assistant." Which actually wasn't true. She tended to take over. And butt in. But maybe she could rein in those tendencies while she kept an eye on him.

"I don't need help," he practically growled at her. And he might not need help, but he hadn't moved since he'd washed up. He was standing in the middle of the kitchen with that lost look on his face again.

"Everyone needs help sometimes," she said gently.

"Fine." As if he couldn't help himself, he lifted his chin toward the industrial sink. "If you're going to help, wash up."

COLT

What was he doing encouraging her to stay? He couldn't do this.

Then he reminded himself: he was helping out a friend who had helped him out. But he was in the last place he ever wanted to be in.

He stood in the industrial kitchen feeling lost. His gaze skimmed over the wiped-down stainless-steel countertops, the deep restaurant sink, and the walk-in refrigerators.

An empty vessel waiting for input.

His fingers twitched and he patted his pocket.

The rich debutante who had haunted his nightly dreams—which frankly was better than his old dreams where he re-lived the worst moment of his life—hovered in the kitchen as if unsure whether to come or go.

Colt resolutely set his chef's skull cap over his hair, surprised at how long it was, curling out the bottom. When he'd been an active restauranteur, he never let the ends get longer than the edge of the cap.

He hadn't picked up a chef's knife in over a year. After agreeing to help out Phoebe when she had an emergency, he hadn't wanted to do so in a crowded kitchen. So he waited until the kitchen was empty, the staff all gone so he could cook in private.

Except *she* was here.

He couldn't decide if it was better that this relative stranger was watching him as he teetered on the edge of panic or if he'd be better off with friends who knew how hard this was and asked him for help anyway.

He needed to do the prep work for a small event tomorrow.

The menu was laid out and the base goods and produce purchased and delivered. All he had to do was cook.

Even that was going to be a challenge.

Colt really didn't want an audience. For several reasons, chief among them he still wasn't sure he could keep down the sandwich he had eaten earlier. Just being in the kitchen was causing his stomach to pitch and roll. Then muscle memory kicked in and Colt's mouth watered. Now, in addition to wanting a cigarette, he really, really wanted a scotch.

Colt was sweating as he placed the squash, carrots, and onions on the stainless-steel prep counter. He slid a cutting board out from a storage slot beneath the counter and put the silicone mat beneath it so that it wouldn't slip.

When he turned around, she was still there.

Deus, he really did not want an audience for this. But he had some weird push-pull fascination with her. And his heart rate settled.

Since she walked into the kitchen, his stress level had plummeted.

Sparring with her kept him from thinking about the fact that he was going to cook again. She clearly had her own problems. He really didn't have a clue why she was waitressing, but if she kept him distracted and focused on cooking rather than on the bar full of bottles in the main dining area and the urgent need to self-medicate, then it was a win.

The look on her face when he took her up on the offer to help was priceless.

"What's the matter, Deb?" Colt put all the vegetables in the large metal colander and washed them, prepping for the next step. A fine dice. "Can't you handle it? If you weren't sincere, then get out. I don't like company."

She snapped her mouth shut, straightened her shoulders, and headed for the sink.

Colt pressed his palms against the cool stainless-steel counter and closed his eyes. He noted the chilled metal beneath his hands.

He listened to the thump of water hitting the bottom of the sink as she scrubbed her hands. He inhaled slowly, and then let it out, searching for a measure of peace.

He could do this.

He had to do this. He had promised.

But damn he sure didn't want to.

The bright overhead light started closing in on him. The therapist he'd gone to right after the incident had a calming technique. Go outside and take in nature. Focus on the horizon.

But it was nighttime and no horizon in sight. His vision narrowed to the tang of the knife, and his scarred fingers clenched around it. Too tightly. He felt like the first time he'd clumsily wielded a chef's knife when he was a kid and hadn't known how to grip it properly or how to cut efficiently and easily.

His heart thundered, pounding so hard that it was all he could hear, like a death knell.

Then her scent, that sweet rose, wormed its way in to his consciousness and calmed him.

"Tell me what to do," she commanded. But her words were soft, gentle.

Once when he'd been in high school, his girlfriend had taken him riding. The stables had been trying to rehabilitate an abused horse. The trainer had soothed the skittish horse with a tone similar to what she was using on him.

She stood next to him waiting patiently.

His hand was shaking as he used the chef's knife to dice the vegetables. They were a mess. Not uniform. Clunky and odd-shaped. He would have ripped a sous chef a new one if they had chopped like this in his kitchen.

Colt paused and tried to get a handle on his seesawing emotions.

He swore creatively. "God bless a cucumber."

Suddenly her soft hand closed over his. "They don't have to be perfect, do they?" She squeezed his hand and let him go.

That innocuous touch was more arousing than full frontal

nudity. Of course that could be a defensive reaction. His body was flooded with adrenaline, which had morphed into arousal and overpowered his fear response. Which would be great if it wasn't so freaking inappropriate.

He cleared his throat and loosened his grip on the knife. "They don't have to be perfect."

"This isn't Boston's restaurant scene. The patrons here like good food and the casual ambience. They will forgive some oddly shaped carrots."

His heart iced. Well that got rid of the stiffy he was sporting. She knew who he was.

Irrelevant right now.

The vegetables would end up pureed in the end. But they wouldn't cook evenly. And he had standards that he wanted to uphold.

However, she was right. No one was judging him. If he kept his name out of it and just cooked this one meal, he could deal. He would handle this and then return to avoiding the kitchen.

As much as he wanted to just ignore her comments, he needed to acknowledge her attempt to help him. He cleared his throat, eased the tightness. "Good point."

It was a damn pot of soup. Not a gourmet meal for four hundred at the White House. No one was going to know he cooked it. He could do this and then slink back to anonymity.

His heart rate settled. Colt grabbed the onions and got to work.

It had been a particularly warm day, and heat had trapped in the walls of the kitchen. During the day, they kept the back door open and the screen door let in a breeze off the river, but tonight everything was already locked up tight.

The kitchen was quiet, peaceful, reminding him of the early days of his career when he would toil extra hours developing new recipes after the restaurant was closed and the staff had all gone home. Experimenting with flavors and textures. Losing himself in the creativity of inventing new food combinations.

Today all he needed to do was make this very simple soup.

A particular calmness settled over him. He could make this work. Having her here was bringing his stress level down. "I need you to measure out flour, butter, and stock." She could get the ingredients for the roux prepped.

"Wait. Don't you have a recipe?"

Some dishes were rote enough that he didn't need one. He hadn't used a recipe for vegetable soup since he was eighteen.

"Nope." Colt's grip on the knife loosened, the hilt comfortable and the heft familiar in his hand, and muscle memory took over and he began to chop with laser precision.

"Not even a blueprint?"

"Just measure out the flour." He told her how much he needed and nudged a large mixing bowl toward her.

"Okay." But she hovered close by, not actually doing what he asked.

"You going to start?"

"Ahh...."

"What now?" He scraped the pile of onions into the large stainless-steel bowl in between them.

"Is there...any specific way I do that?"

She didn't know how to measure.

"You really are a deb."

She bristled. "I just excel at other things," she said loftily. "I'd like to see you coordinate a fundraiser for seven hundred and fifty people." She firmed her mouth.

He stepped away from his chopping and showed her how to measure. Placing his hands over hers. Again that sizzle of attraction fizzed in his bloodstream, giving him a heady feeling.

They broke apart awkwardly.

"What's this for?" she asked.

"A small fundraiser for the local food bank. The gastropub is giving out samples at tomorrow's Colebury Farmers Market." Soup and the restaurant's pretzel rolls. He could make this in his sleep. Except he rarely slept much.

After the last year, he frequently lay awake and wondered where he went wrong. Everything was tied up in the kitchen and fame. And chasing that fame.

The spotlight was a toxic place and he wanted nothing to do with it. Staying out of the kitchen ensured that no one bothered him, and he couldn't spiral into destructive patterns again. His plan for the past year had been working, and removing himself from the tools of his destruction had granted him a measure of peace.

But that peace had been disrupted by several things lately: Phoebe and Audrey asking him to cater for the Speakeasy. The arrival of this woman who epitomized all the people whose approval he'd been chasing. He should want her gone; instead he was inexplicably drawn to her.

"Ooh." She clapped her hands, her blue eyes sparkling. "You should serve the soup in little paper cups with the pretzel rolls on the side and a little flag, with information for donating on the flag." She got a faraway look in her eyes.

Colt held his hands up in surrender. "I'm just the substitute cook."

"It would be super easy to set it up."

"Pretty sure people will just give a ten spot when they pick up their order."

"You need to have vehicles for them to remember the organization, so they'll see that little tag and consider donating again." She pulled out her phone and looked up the website. "I can make the flags on my printer. It will be super easy. And I can use toothpicks from the bar to wrap the flags around." She tapped something into her phone. "Can I take a picture of you?"

"No."

His response had been immediate and harsh.

She looked taken aback. "Umm, okay?"

"Absolutely no pictures."

"What about of the kitchen? And the prep? And maybe your hands?"

His hands?

"Fine," he grumbled. "No one wants to see pictures of food prep."

"You'd be surprised." Cee-Cee bustled happily around the kitchen, snapping pictures on her phone with a studied efficiency, moving the bowls and the knives to capture the proper lighting. "People like behind-the-scenes glimpses of things. They like feeling like they are included in something."

His restaurant group had had social media accounts. And they'd encouraged patrons to post pictures. Back then he'd been obsessed with fame. He hadn't run the accounts but his assistant had given him regular updates about likes and retweets. Even when he'd been chasing fame, he'd thought that social media exposure only provided minimal benefit.

"If we tag it properly, we can get more eyeballs on the fundraiser." She bounced on her toes.

"It's just a small fundraiser." He was compelled to reiterate the purpose.

When he worked in Boston, his restaurant group had partnered with several food insecurity philanthropies to distribute groceries and leftover meals to local homeless shelters.

He was all for wiping out hunger.

And he personally had donated time and his brain power to work on a major fundraiser in Boston. He'd forgotten about the more positive memories of his fame—raising money because people had come out to see him.

"Cool." She snapped a few more photos. "I'll research whether the farmers market has social media handles. As well as the food bank and the town." She chattered on about viral posts and ways to increase views as she flitted around the kitchen.

He thought about asking her if she was planning on helping but her voice lulled him into a zone as he chopped away.

"You know, if you have an account, you could post on your account. You'd be a big draw."

"Absolutely not." He put the knife down carefully and tamped down on his temper. She didn't know what she was asking. "No publicity," he said resolutely. "For me. Or about me."

She stopped, paused, studied him with somber blue eyes. "Okay." Finally she tucked her phone away. "Hit me with what to do."

Colt's curiosity got the better of him. "Why are you here?" He couldn't figure her out.

"I'm helping you cook, silly."

She projected this air of affability and light. Except Colt saw beyond that public face. She had walls a mile high and he bet people rarely saw the real her.

"Why are you in Colebury?" he clarified, wondering what the hell he was doing. He hated it when people interfered in his life. But he couldn't stop wondering, so he was compelled to find out more.

Her smile slipped. "I'm just taking a break from my life."

Something in her tone alarmed him. "Are you in danger?"

"No. Of course not." But Cee-Cee frowned. "Just trying out a change of scenery."

"Well, you'll definitely find that here." Colt had grown up in Connecticut in a small city called Danbury. And then he had lived in various cities in the Northeast. Coming to the country had been culture shock. But he'd adjusted to the slower pace of life and the fact that in small rural towns people were up in each other's business constantly.

The tension that gripped him eased. "Okay." She had secrets. He understood that. They were none of his business. He didn't want to know them anyway.

Right?

But the niggle of curiosity was like a tickle at the back of his throat that wouldn't go away.

The soup was finished.

Colt cleaned up the kitchen, wiping down the counters with disinfectant and scrubbing the utensils with the industrial soap. There weren't enough utensils to run the dishwasher so he was washing everything by hand. Old habits died hard and he didn't want to use unnecessary utilities and drive up the restaurant's overhead costs. Cee-Cee grabbed a towel to dry. He handed her the utensils after he rinsed.

He realized he'd been in the kitchen for a few hours. The bar beyond the doors was silent. Grace, the jazz singer, had packed up and left over an hour ago. And the last bartender had popped his head in to say goodnight then headed out not long after her. Which meant that he and Cee-Cee were alone in the restaurant.

His hands were pleasantly sore and he settled into the familiarity of late-night kitchen sounds and scents. The odor of flour and herbs scented the air along with the aromatic soup. He'd tweaked the recipe and added a little turmeric and ginger for color and flavor and to boost immunity.

She yawned as she wiped down the counters, spraying them liberally with cleaner. He decided to mess with her. "You going to do the bathrooms next?"

She stopped mid-swipe and looked at him with wide eyes. Panicked.

"Standard operating procedure, kitchen cleanup also is responsible for the bathrooms."

"Umm."

The look on her face was priceless. He laughed, from deep in his belly. Laughter bubbled up, cramping his stomach, he bent over, picturing her momentary horror.

"You should do that more often," she said softly. Her smile grew, the amusement spreading over her face self-deprecating. "You were kidding."

"Yep. They have a cleaning service who comes in and cleans the bathrooms and other areas." He collected all the dirty linens and dropped them in the industrial laundry bin so they'd be ready to be sent out tomorrow. "Restaurants are notorious for pranks. If you're going to stay here, you better get used to it."

She leaned against the stainless-steel counter and crossed her arms. "Really?"

The lights were bright, illuminating her face. It was amazing that she still looked good. Her shirt was rumpled and her jeans had a swath of flour over one hip. Even though it was late, her skin glowed with a singular beauty and her eyes sparkled, making him feel like he was the only person in the universe. She had a unique ability to give people a sense that they were special. That she valued them. He'd noticed the similar reaction from her customers yesterday. She made people feel good.

He put the industrial pots of soup in the large walk-in refrigerator. "Let me do one last check and then I'll walk you out."

"There's a closing checklist in Phoebe's office."

Colt snickered. He could close down a restaurant in his sleep. "I've got it."

They walked into the darkened restaurant and checked to make sure the front doors were locked. Colt turned off the lights, leaving the security light that illuminated the parking lot on.

Cee-Cee yawned so wide her jaw cracked.

"Waitressing getting to you."

"It's the combination of working all day then waitressing at night. I had no idea how hard it would be," she said absently as she tugged on the front door one more time.

Working? "Why are you working here then?"

"I'm a little short on cash," she said reluctantly. She glanced at the Cartier watch on her wrist. "It's only eleven thirty. In the city, I would just be going out now." Her laughter was a light waterfall of sound that Colt wanted to bathe in.

"How are you getting home?"

"I've got my car."

"I'll follow you."

"Not really worried about the mean streets of Colebury," she teased. But her smile was soft, welcoming, pleased.

Somehow in the past few hours, she'd mellowed his mood.

She stood next to him in the yellow glow of the security spotlight by the back door. Colt locked up quickly and turned. She was closer than he anticipated, and he almost bumped into her.

Her rose scent surrounded him. "How do you still smell so fabulous?"

"I've got a small spritzer in my bag." She lifted the leather hobo bag with the designer logo, her sterling silver charm bracelet sliding along her arm, the pavé diamond Eiffel Tower charm resting on her forearm. "I have it made in Paris."

That should throw cold water on his attraction. She had bespoke perfume designed in France.

But instead, he said, "God, I love Paris." Colt closed his eyes and remembered the thrill of Paris. He'd worked in a venerated restaurant under one of the most famous chefs at the time and lived in a tiny atelier on the top floor of the building. The long days and nights had been a formative experience.

"I know, right?"

"The food. The history. The sheer energy." He had a flash of them sitting at a quintessential Parisian café as the motorcycles roared by, sharing a plate of brie and a fresh baguette, and the sun shimmering through a sparkling rose.

She leaned against the brick exterior of the old mill building as he locked up. A dreamy smile on her face, her eyes half closed. Her lush scent surrounded him.

He had the unsettling urge to kiss her.

It had been a really long time since he'd kissed a woman. Since he'd had his meltdown.

His last girlfriend had up and left him when he was no longer a celebrity. And after she was gone he'd realized how shallow their relationship actually was. She was a model who'd barely eaten his food and complained about his hours.

His last kiss had been over a year ago. She'd rage-kissed him, tossed her high-maintenance hair that took over an hour to perfect, and then told him she was too good for him.

At the time she hadn't been wrong.

But now the urge to wipe away that memory burned in his brain. To replace it with the soft lips and happy smile of Cee-Cee the waitress.

Colt blinked. Stepped away. Bad idea. On so many levels.

He was a still a mess. And she was a woman running from something. He didn't need complications in his life. He'd retreated to the country to heal and to hide.

He'd survived his first time back in the kitchen.

But he wasn't ready for anything else.

7

COLT

Early the next evening, Colt walked into the Speakeasy kitchen, bypassing the front door and going through the employee entrance.

"Dude. Great idea for the little tags on the pretzel rolls." The director of the food bank, Noah, was unloading the empty soup pots into the large sink, his normal laid-back attitude nowhere to be seen. He practically vibrated with happiness.

"Wasn't me," Colt grunted, sorry he'd come into the restaurant today. "It was the waitress, Cee-Cee."

"You mean the absolutely awful waitress?"

Colt grinned. "Yep." She was terrible. But she managed to charm the customers anyway. "Customers seem to love her."

They weren't the only ones.

Colt would never admit it but there was an anticipation in his step as he idly, or not so idly, wondered if she would be here. She was like a giant ball of light and he was the moth drawn to her sun.

"Well, I love her too. We sold out of the soup and rolls and in addition to the cash we raised at the farmers market, we also brought in more money on our website," he gushed. "She posted a picture of the soup, roll, and flag on her Instagram account. Some hashtag she used was genius and now we've taken in double what we were expecting."

Colt raised his eyebrows. "Seriously?"

"Yes!" Noah nodded so hard his blond man bun wobbled.

The kitchen was bustling with the waitstaff who ebbed and flowed around them as they chatted. He glanced toward the dining room only half his attention on their conversation. "That's great news."

"Right?" Noah said slyly, "She's here."

"Who?"

"The woman of the hour."

Colt flushed, hoping his tan would hide the physiological reaction to seeing her again. He could feel heat roll through him. "I wasn't asking."

But once he saw her, he found himself headed to her location anyway.

She sat at a table in the corner, muttering and staring at her computer screen.

"Someone doxing you on Facebook?" Colt joked when she didn't look up but continued to be hyperfocused on whatever she was working on.

She jerked her head up, her blue eyes wide. "Oh. Uh, hello." She shut her laptop quickly.

Anne set a club soda at her side.

"Oh, hey can you ask the bartender for a lemon?" Cee-Cee asked. "I forgot to."

"Sure."

Colt watched as Demetrio flirted with Anne. Then he studied Cee-Cee, who had a too-satisfied smile on her face. "You don't drink lemon in your water."

"What?" She blinked. "I'm sure I do."

The day he'd first seen her, she'd very deliberately fished the lemon out of her water and set it on her plate without squeezing it.

He raised a brow, basically signaling "liar, liar, pants on fire." "No, you don't."

"You actually pay attention to what people drink?"

More than she'd know. And not necessarily everyone, but definitely gorgeous women who caught his attention. He said piously, "Good restauranteurs catalogue everything about their customers."

Now she raised a dark blond brow at him. "Really?"

He'd been very good at his job. Until he wasn't. "What are you up to?"

"Nothing."

Anne bopped back to the table. "Can you work for me tonight?"

"Oh," Cee-Cee glanced back at her closed laptop. "Sure."

"Demetrio asked me out!"

"That's great." Cee-Cee beamed at the waitress.

"Anything else?" Anne asked.

There was an empty plate on the table along with a crumpled-up napkin. "No. I'm good for now."

"What are you doing here?" Colt asked when he realized she wasn't on shift right now.

"The motor lodge doesn't have room service."

He laughed. But at the somber expression on her face, he figured out she wasn't kidding. "Roughing it is tough."

Cee-Cee frowned at her laptop. "You have no idea," she muttered.

He should just leave her alone with whatever she was working on and walk away. But he found himself lingering. "You posted on social media?" He couldn't keep the disdain out of his voice.

"Just trying to increase donations," she said defensively. "And raise awareness."

"Well, thank you." As much as it pained him and as much as he was not a fan of social media, she had helped raise the profile of the organization. It wasn't her fault that he wanted nothing to do with promotion or the spotlight.

"You're welcome."

Ty Connor, the bar manager of the Speakeasy, approached him. "Hey. It's Colton, right?"

Colt had seen Ty around but beyond a chin lift to acknowledge him as a local they hadn't really spoken.

"Yeah." He sounded grumpy. He'd only stopped by to have a meal with Phoebe and sure, if Cee-Cee was around, he'd figured he'd talk to her.

"Great. Glad you're here." Ty said it as if he was expecting Colt. But for what?

Ugh. This was why he didn't come into town. Damn Phoebe and Audrey for getting him out here. And damn, Cee-Cee for being so intriguing that he'd gone against his better instincts and come back. Several times.

Ty thrust out his hand and introduced himself formally. "Phoebe just called and said you would be here to meet the customers who booked the fiftieth wedding anniversary party for upstairs."

Colt just stared. "You've got the wrong guy."

"You're not a chef?"

"Fifty years!" Cee-Cee clasped her hands in front of her, her eyes wide with amazement. "Can you imagine?"

"No." His voice and tone were harsh. He didn't give a rat's ass about wedding anniversaries. *And what the hell, Phoebe?*

Her face fell. "You don't think it's amazing?"

He tuned out Cee-Cee and turned to Ty. "I'm not the chef."

"But you're an excellent chef," Cee-Cee interjected. "He made the soup for the food bank fundraiser. Everyone said it was fabulous."

He shushed her. He didn't want to cook.

"The clients will be here in a few minutes. Did I misunderstand?"

"Yes."

"Okay." Ty walked away and pulled out his cell.

Colt could feel the walls closing in on him. But then Cee-Cee pulled his attention away from his mini freak-out.

"Fifty years." She had a dreamy expression on her face. "What do you supposed it's like to spend that much time with one person?"

"Jail."

"What?" She looked like he'd kicked her puppy. Then she sighed. "I supposed you're right. There's probably some awful secret in their past or even their present. This is probably just social restitution for a horrible wrong they perpetrated on each other."

Wow, he thought he was cynical but that was borderline scathing and contemptuous. She slumped over the table, her chin in her hand.

"Bad breakup?" He couldn't believe he'd asked. But that would explain the mystery of her presence in Colebury. And dammit, he didn't want to be intrigued. But he definitely was. That would also explain the contempt she'd just leveled on the yet-to-appear happy couple.

Her face fell.

Shit. Why would he ask that? As far as he could tell she was happily trying to set up everyone in the bar but herself.

"Not recently. Not ever, actually." Cee-Cee smiled sadly. "I don't think marriage is for me."

But her voice was melancholy, and sadness seemed to seep from her pores. As if she longed for that connection but didn't think she'd ever have it. He wanted to erase that look from her face. Banish the sadness from her eyes. He found he couldn't bear for her to be unhappy.

She distracted him by asking, "What about you?"

"Divorced."

"Really?" She shook her head, eyebrows raised in surprise. "Must have been amiable."

Normally he wouldn't share so much but that sad look was gone. Replaced by curiosity.

"I should have been more torn up about it but honestly, getting married had been a whim." Which was never a good idea. Back in his wild days when he'd burned bright and hot. "Wife couldn't handle the hours or my stress level."

She also hadn't been a fan of his drinking. She'd managed to get her digs in at him, when he'd had his meltdown. She made the rounds of the talk show circuits talking about his volatile mood swings and uneven temper. Which was ironic since she was the one who'd thrown things when they'd decided to get divorced.

The worst part had been the disappointment of his parents. Which pretty much said everything about how much he'd loved his wife. Not enough.

His Mami and Papi were devout Catholics. They hated that he'd gotten divorced even though they weren't big fans of his ex-wife.

"I'm sorry." Now she looked distressed.

"Ancient history." He wasn't lying when he said he really wasn't torn up about it. Which was a big fat clue right there that he hadn't been invested the way he should have been. He'd gotten married on a whim. The divorce proceedings had lasted longer than their entire relationship.

Speaking of relationships, right now he needed to deal with the potential client coming in.

"Where are you going?" Cee-Cee called after him.

"To make a phone call."

He stepped through the kitchen and out the side door. Before he could dial his friend, his phone rang. The readout had Phoebe's name.

"I've been trying to call you." She sounded out of breath. "Are you at the Speakeasy?"

They'd had plans to meet so she could thank him for doing the soup.

"Let me guess. It's about the fiftieth wedding anniversary."

"Oh crap. They are there."

"Apparently they will be here in a minute."

"Look, I never meant to back you into a corner. I just got held up," Phoebe begged. "If you stall them, I'll be there as fast as I can."

"I'll take care of it."

Silence on the other end. "Um you aren't known for your tact."

He laughed. "True. I'll have Cee-Cee help."

"She's a terrible waitress," Phoebe commented.

"But she's excellent with customers and apparently has experience with planning large events." Colt brushed off Phoebe's concerns.

"Really?"

"So she claims."

"I don't know what she's running from but—"

"She isn't dangerous," Colt finished. She exuded sunshine and puppies but not anything worrisome. She had secrets. He got that. But whatever she was hiding was no threat to anyone here.

Except maybe to the tough, grumpy exterior shell he'd cultivated over the past year.

8

TRACY

Tracy chased after Ty. She didn't know him well. He was usually busy keeping the bar stocked and managing the bartenders. He never seemed to stop moving. "What can I do to help?"

"Cee-Cee, right?"

She nodded.

"You aren't working right now."

Tracy shook her head. "No. "

"You cook?" He eyed her speculatively.

Tracy laughed nervously. She could fake her way through a lot of things, but cooking wasn't one of them. "Nope. But I'm golden at planning."

"That's perfect since it's their golden anniversary."

Fifty years. That was amazing.

"Holy moly. Fifty years." A happy warmth spread through her. Her mission in life was to help people find their happily every afters. This time she'd be able to help celebrate one.

The happy couple, who looked to be in their late sixties or early seventies, walked into the dining area. Wow, they must have been young when they got married.

Oh my gosh. They were holding hands. How sweet was that?

Tracy's heart grew like the grinch's.

The portly older man wore painter jeans with loops on the sides to hold brushes and hammers and other tools, and a short-sleeved plaid shirt. A tape measure was hooked on his belt loop and a stretchy metal watch band with a round old-fashioned face circled his thick wrist. He was balding on top, had mixed salt-and-pepper hair, more salt than pepper, and ruddy cheeks with a wide smile. Next to him was a plump woman with a rosy complexion and white hair curled up like a character from the old seventies show *Charlie's Angels*, and held back with little pastel pink butterfly clips. She wore floral shorts and a pink short-sleeved top with embroidered lace on the pockets that matched her hair clips.

Fifty years was so hard to imagine. The commitment. The love. The fortitude to be together for that long and still want to cele-brate. She'd been a little cynical while talking to Colt, but truth-fully she wanted to believe that this couple was truly happy.

"Hi! I'm Cee-Cee." Tracy thrust out her hand.

"Lottie and Chuck." The woman introduced them both.

Tracy shook their hands and then gestured to the chairs at the table. "Have a seat."

She could entertain in her sleep. She'd been born schmoozing, and making this couple feel comfortable was totally in her wheel-house. "Would you like something to eat while we discuss your ideas for the anniversary party?" She handed them a menu. Once they told her what they wanted, she wrote up an order. "I'll be right back."

Tracy dropped an order on the counter between the dining room and the kitchen and hoped she saw Colt so she could give him a piece of her mind.

As if she conjured him up, he was coming out of the manag-er's office.

Tracy had an opportunity here. She was practiced at smoothing things over, but right now she didn't want to make things easier for him. She was going to give him a piece of her mind. In Boston, she would work the room and work the details and create the spin to make her father and his political organization look their best. She was tired of it. She wanted to be who she wanted. She didn't want to be that passive and deferential anymore.

She marched toward him.

"Listen here." She poked him in the chest and then blinked. His muscles contracted against her jab. Damn, he had a gorgeous chest. And hard muscles.

He raised his eyebrows, a smirk on his mouth. And her brain automatically shifted to sex.

Dammit she needed to stay focused on her message. "Those people are here to talk about their anniversary celebration, and you are going to sit down and converse with them. You can work out the details of who is going to cook it later."

He waited until there was a break in her diatribe. "Okay."

She opened her mouth to continue her argument. Wait, what?

COLT

Colt wanted to laugh at the look of consternation on her face. "I was planning on coming back."

"You were?" She closed her mouth.

He thought it might be the quietest he'd ever seen her. She was in constant motion, always gesturing with her hands and moving with her words.

He might not want to be the catering chef and there might be some sort of miscommunication, but he wasn't about to leave a Speakeasy customer hanging.

He owed so much to his friends and his family. Wasn't that why he quit? To protect everyone from his destructive behavior. A protector wouldn't abandon his friends. He had no desire to go back in the kitchen, but he also wouldn't screw his friends over.

"However, I would appreciate it if you would join the meeting with me. I don't have much experience with catering gigs."

She hadn't said a word, just continued to stare at him with a bemused look on her face. Then she nodded.

"Let's get to it." Colt headed for the dining room.

Cee-Cee introduced Colt to the older couple and they got down to the nitty-gritty so they could nail down specifics for the party.

"What made you decided to have a party?" Cee-Cee asked.

"Well...." Lottie blushed. "We eloped at seventeen the first time. So we just want a modest little party to celebrate fifty years."

"Fifty years is amazing." She clapped her hands. "First let's talk food."

Colt was happy to let her take over. She was better with people anyway.

Chuck cleared his throat. "Family style. That way picky eaters aren't locked in to eating things they don't want."

That would be easier.

"And there's less waste." Cee-Cee nodded as if Chuck had suggested a community-wide composting party. "Do you have any favorite foods? What did you have for dinner the night you got married?"

"McDonald's. That was all we could afford."

"What if we did appetizers that played on the McDonald's menu? Sliders, chicken tenders, French fries."

He might as well go to Costco and graze the frozen aisle.

Colt frowned at the jolt of energy that buzzed through him. No way were they having Costco appetizers. He could do small bites with twists on the sauces and some unusual ingredients for the sliders. Beef with horseradish sauce and caramelized onions. Pulled pork with plum barbeque sauce and a spicy slaw. Maybe a banh mi.

If he spiced up the batter for the chicken tenders, he could fry up several different flavors with complementary sauces.

Truffle fries. Cheese curd fries, maybe a play on a poutine.

His mind was racing with ideas. The creative burn of excitement flooded through him.

"But of course it will be a fancier version. The chefs at the Speakeasy are phenomenal." Cee-Cee shot a proud look at Colt and he shoved down the desire to preen. "Any foods you particularly love for the main dish?"

"Well...I do love prime rib."

Lottie fretted. "It isn't good for your cholesterol."

"Once won't hurt."

"I want you around for the next fifty years." She leaned over and squeezed her husband's hand and rested her head on his shoulder.

Cee-Cee nearly melted into a puddle next to him. Jeez, she was a soft touch.

Chuck wrapped his arm around Lottie's shoulder. "Okay, maybe no prime rib."

Colt could tell that Chuck was disappointed. "What if we do family style platters with several options? One with steak medallions with a red wine demi-glace and another with a savory chicken or turkey dish with a maple mustard glaze?"

"That would probably work," Lottie said softly.

"What's the date? We can choose side dishes that make the most of the freshest ingredients and focus on local produce." Colt was mentally ticking through some of his signature vegetable dishes. He could share the recipes with Phoebe. Several local artisanal farms had sprung up over the past few years. "We could do a salad with Mason Rye's Garden Goat and Dairy Farm goat cheese and figs and a local balsamic and Lyon honey dressing."

He was composing dishes in his head, his creativity like overflowing like a burst pipe.

"That sounds...delightful." Lottie's eyes lit up.

Cee-Cee interrupted his recipe tangent. "Are you going to have a cake?"

"We hadn't really thought about cake," Lottie demurred.

"I'll bet Oh for Heaven's Cakes can make something special," Cee-Cee said. "Gigi Hawthorne is a genius."

Colt raised his eyebrows. She'd been in town for all of a few days and she already knew the local bakery?

"Any specifics? Do you have a favorite flavor? Flowers on the cake, real or frosting?" Cee-Cee made some notes on a pad next to her computer. She shot more questions at them and scribbled furiously.

"We just want something simple," Lottie said softly but there was a yearning in her eyes that belied the statement.

"I want you to be happy," Chuck said firmly. "We did simple fifty years ago. We survived through kids and financial struggles and births and deaths and taxes. We need to celebrate that achievement."

Lottie's eyes sparkled. "Whatever you want dear."

Colt reassessed his initial assumption that this party was for Lottie. Suddenly he wasn't sure if the big to-do was more for Chuck than Lottie.

Cee-Cee asked a few more preliminary questions about linens and drinks and decorations. Colt tuned out the alcohol discussion.

Cee-Cee asked, "So what's your secret?"

"What secret?" They both looked bewildered.

"To staying together all these years."

"Stubbornness doesn't hurt." But Lottie laughed when she said it.

"Respect. Honoring the things we both do to be a united team."

Lottie grabbed his hand and twined their fingers together.

"Doesn't it piss you off when he leaves the toilet seat up?" Cee-Cee teased.

Colt laughed out loud. Didn't every couple fight about the toilet seat?

"He learned not to do that real fast." Lottie gave Chuck a look of affection so pure that it caused a lump in his throat.

Cee-Cee prodded Chuck. "What about when she cooks something she knows you don't like but it's good for you?"

"She's just looking out for me. Although I will never like broccoli." Chuck whispered in Cee-Cee's ear, "Don't tell her, but I hide it in my napkin and throw it away when she isn't looking."

"I'm always looking out for you." Lottie leaned in. "And I know he throws it away. But I'll never give up trying to keep him healthy."

They all laughed.

Cee-Cee seemed to draw out the best in people. Even Chuck and Lottie blossomed under her attention.

"Well, we will get these notes typed up."

Colt should have interjected that Phoebe would be in touch, but he was reluctant to verbally pass them off to someone else.

He and Cee-Cee waved as Chuck and Lottie left the Speakeasy with giant smiles on their faces. Colt thought Chuck had an extra bounce in his step, happy that Lottie was finally getting the wedding reception she'd dreamed of. Or maybe the wedding reception he'd always dreamed of. Because he'd been just as full of ideas as his wife.

Cee-Cee turned and smiled at Colt. "How exciting! Their relationship is beautiful."

Colt grunted.

"C'mon you have to admit they are super cute."

Super cute? "What are we, in middle school?"

TRACY

Tracy frowned at him, trying to tamp down her irritation. "Admit they were adorable."

He grudgingly agreed. "Fine. They do seem very happy. Get any good tips?" Colt teased.

"Well, my partner won't need to worry about me cooking him something he doesn't like. There's one future argument avoided."

He laughed.

"Fifty years." Cee-Cee rested her chin on her fist and sighed, dreamily. "What an amazing accomplishment." She'd been too busy facilitating "happily ever after" for other people. She sighed again, her euphoria disintegrating in a sea of disillusionment. How would she ever find that fairy tale when she couldn't be honest about her life?

And who would ever want the scrutiny and headaches that came with being a member of a political family?

She had baggage the size of a steamer trunk. She'd need a decade to unpack it.

But seeing that couple, so obviously in love with each other—still!—after so many years was both inspiring and incredibly saddening.

"What's wrong?"

"Why do you think something is wrong?"

"You are projecting."

She kept a vapid smile on her face. "You must be mistaken."

"Don't think I am." Then he did the oddest thing. He reached his hand, scarred and nicked, rough with calluses, and placed it over hers. His touch was warm, comforting. Sweet. Offering her a small gift. "You did good, Cee-Cee."

Her heart expanded filling her chest like a balloon with helium. It was the first time he called her by name, her fake name, but still.

"You feeling okay?" she teased.

"Why do you ask?"

"You are being awfully sweet."

"No one has ever accused me of being sweet." His voice was gruff, embarrassed.

"Why'd you come meet with Lottie and Chuck?"

"Phoebe asked me to."

"So you were looking out for your friend."

"Sure."

"That's really nice." There was an awkward pause.

"Nice and sweet." Colt rolled his eyes. "That's me."

COLT

Colt hated to see her looking sad. Her joy lit up a room. And without it the day felt unbearably gray.

He'd cut off his left nut before he admitted that to anyone. However his current goal was to bring a smile back to her face. "Let's go for a walk."

She blinked at him. "You want to go for a walk?"

"I've been reading a nonfiction book on neuroscience. Getting outside is good for the soul."

"You think my soul is in need of goodness?"

He wasn't touching that one. "It will clear your head before you start your shift."

Cee-Cee stowed her laptop, state-of-the-art and expensive, in a locker in the employee break room.

They snuck out the employee side entrance and Colt led her to the path along the Winooski River.

An air of melancholy surrounded her. "Why so blue?" he asked.

"You ever want something so badly that you bypass all reason and forget all logic in your quest to achieve it?"

As much as he hated delving into her issues, he thought she needed it. He didn't have any desire to be her therapist. But what she was describing sounded like him two years ago. He'd forsaken everything in his obsession to become a famous chef. Then he'd ingested alcohol and cigarettes to fuel his ambitions, winding tighter and tighter until he'd snapped.

He wondered if she was about to reveal why she was in Colebury and what she was doing in a small town hiding when she was clearly a city girl with a rich life and many connections. He shuddered. He really shouldn't want to find out what drove her.

Right now he liked her. Grudgingly. "What is it you want that you're willing to do anything to get?"

"That perfection Chuck and Lottie had." Cee-Cee waved her arm toward the Speakeasy. "But we know that's a myth, right?"

Relationships. She was talking about a relationship. Not some blind aggressive ambition to succeed in business.

While he had not experienced love like Chuck and Lottie, he thought about his family. "My parents make it work. I mean they fight, and sometimes it's loud and chaotic. But they also always make up. It's like…a release rather than a battle."

What would it be like to share in life's troubles and its triumphs? And why the hell was he thinking about that now? The last thing he needed was someone else to worry about. He was still working through his own issues and dealing with his lingering neuroses. But he was curious about her. "What's stopping you from reaching for that kind of relationship?"

She didn't answer right away. "I'd rather help other people."

But he knew that wasn't completely true or she wouldn't have brought it up. "Why can't you also help yourself?"

"I can't imagine ever being so vulnerable with a man." She gave him a side glance.

When he thought of her sharing her innermost thoughts and feelings with another man, he was uncomfortable with how much he hated the idea of her with someone else. "If it's something you really want, then you have to reach for it."

At least she knew what she wanted. Lately he'd been floundering, hiding, and not moving forward. Stuck in place. Afraid to start dreaming and wanting again. In the past he'd had too many goals and ambitions, and now he didn't have any.

"Yeah, well. That kind of connection is rare," she said wistfully. "Plenty of people pretend that their marriage is perfect, but the truth is, it's rotten beneath the surface."

Wow. Again with the unexpected negativity. That cynicism threw him off balance. She always appeared to be an eternal optimist. Someone must have hurt her badly. How could he cheer her up?

"Rotten, huh?" Colt teased. "Aren't you the Debbie Downer."

"No one has ever accused me of that before."

He'd bet.

They walked further away from the bustle and noise of the Speakeasy kitchen. The river gurgled in the background.

As if she had just tracked into their conversation from earlier, she said, "You read?"

He snorted. "Yeah."

He hadn't in the past. He hadn't had time. But the transition from the frenetic pace of owning several restaurants, competing on chef shows, to living in a quiet cabin in the woods had enabled him to make time for things he'd forsaken.

"Trying to figure myself out," he confessed.

"Reaching for your higher self?"

"Something like that." Trying hard not to repeat the mistakes from the past.

9

COLT

Colt found himself back at the Speakeasy.

He'd been at home and the silence of his little cabin had been oppressive. He'd paced the small area, tried to read a book on self-improvement, even tried to get a little work done.

For the first few months, he'd just hibernated in the cabin and wallowed. But eventually he needed a job and income and frankly, something to do.

His new gig was freelance editing and ghost writing cookbooks. He wasn't testing the recipes. He just looked over proportions and judged if they were correct. So far, he hadn't run across any that seemed out of balance.

But lately he couldn't seem to focus on anything. He was antsy and out of sorts.

He spirited in through the employee entrance and headed toward an empty table. Dusk was falling. A scruffy guy with a guitar sat on a stool lit by a single spotlight, crooning a lonely folk song.

He sat at one of the two tops near the stage. He couldn't

believe he was back here again. But he couldn't seem to stay away.

Colt's gaze automatically searched for Cee-Cee.

But she wasn't there.

He ate a quick dinner and then left, surprised at the level of disappointment when he realized he wouldn't see her.

He stopped off at the tractor supply store on his way home for more gardening supplies. On his way to the correct aisle, he glanced at the clothing wall, remembering his encounter with her and he laughed. She'd been convinced those little ballet flats were fine. However she'd been wearing supportive but far less fashionable shoes the last time he saw her at the Speakeasy. Everywhere he turned, small snippets of their conversations came back to him.

On his way to register, he saw her distinctive cap of blond hair.

He paused, noting her unnatural stillness as she stood in front of a wall of cleaning supplies. Based on her horror when he'd mentioned cleaning the bathroom, he couldn't imagine what she was looking for.

Just thinking about her response caused him to smile.

He headed toward her, a lightness in his heart, as if he'd conjured her up from his daydreams.

He was about to tease her when he saw the very clear distress on her face. "Everything okay?"

"I have no idea which one to buy."

This wasn't Costco. The choices were relatively limited.

"I need to do laundry," she whispered, "It shouldn't be hard. Right?"

"How dirty?"

"Work clothes. I've been handwashing in the sink every day but after a long shift they really need a more in-depth cleaning." She looked completely out of her element. She touched each of the detergents with a light fingertip. "Which one is best?"

He studied her three options and then chose the best one. "This is what I would use."

"Thanks."

"I'm not usually this indecisive," she clarified.

He figured her to be in her late twenties. "Haven't you ever done laundry?"

She snorted.

Once again he wondered what kind of background she came from. She had the bearing of a woman used to a certain level of comfort. She was obviously wealthy and certainly privileged. Seriously, why was she waitressing in Vermont?

"Thanks for your help," she said softly. She gripped the plastic bottle tightly as if she were hanging on by a thread. Uncertainty surrounded her like a cloud.

"You want a lesson?"

He heard himself make the offer, his mouth talking before his brain could catch up. But he felt lighter as soon as he made the offer. He could have told her to read the directions. He was sure there were videos on YouTube or the internet that would show her how. But she seemed so alone.

"That would be...nice."

"You're gonna need quarters."

She looked at him blankly.

"To pay for the machines," Colt said.

Her eyes widened and her mouth formed an O.

For some reason, he found her ineptitude cute. Clearly he was losing his mind. But Colt followed her back to the motor lodge anyway.

TRACY

Tracy was the first to admit that she was thrilled to have help.

The graying linoleum in the laundry room of the motor lodge had probably been stylish and new in the sixties. Now it was just a dingy reminder that many feet had shuffled through this room throughout the years.

There were two orange hard plastic chairs near the door to the small room. A small table between the chairs held old copies of *People* magazine and various tabloid papers. Tracy clutched the paper grocery store bag that doubled as a laundry hamper in her arms.

There were three washers and three dryers.

She couldn't believe she'd agreed to let him help her with the laundry. She could figure it out on her own. Of course she could. She wasn't an idiot.

But she was lonely.

"I could do this on my own," she felt compelled to explain.

"I know." But there was an indulgent tone to his voice that caused her hackles to rise.

"I graduated at the top of my class at Boston College in marketing and neuroscience." She should be able to remember a flipping lunch order. And she could definitely follow laundry directions.

"Congratulations."

"It's not like I'm a simpleton."

"No one said you were."

"I could totally figure this out."

"Do you want my help or not?" He sounded exasperated.

"Yes. I'm sorry. I don't like feeling out of my element." And the past week had been one long "let's poke Tracy where she was most vulnerable" fest. Cut off from her family, as annoying as they could be, and her friends, she was adrift. She hadn't realized how much she counted on her support network until she didn't have one anymore.

"No one does," he said mildly. "Put your clothes in."

She dumped the whole bag in at once.

"Hold up." He raised his palm. "Don't mix the dark and light. Didn't you watch the *Friends* episode where Rachel turned her whites pink?"

"Nope." She'd been too busy learning table etiquette and memorizing the names of dignitaries' kids.

"Okay. Lesson number one. Put like colors together. Separate into light and dark."

He opened the lid of the machine next to the one she'd already dumped her clothes in.

Tracy picked out the whites, flushing at the lacy bra and panty combo.

"Nice undies." His voice was gravelly.

She tossed them in the second machine quickly and finished separating the dark and light colors.

"Choose your temperature."

"Does that have something to do with fabric type?"

"Chef—" he held up his hands "—not fashion designer. I just throw everything in on cold water. Except my sheets. Those I wash on hot."

Sheets brought up beds. Suddenly Tracy had a vision of him wrapped in white sheets, his tan limbs and dark hair a striking contrast, lean body, muscles on display. The sexy image burned in her brain, and the daydreams she'd had of him came roaring back.

She cleared her throat. "Okay. So cold water works." She set the temperature.

"Now you need the quarters."

She pulled out her phone and frowned, pressing her phone to the top of the washing machine. "No TouchPay?" Her mouth twitched with amusement.

He opened his mouth to blast her and then stopped. "I see what you did there."

Now she was the one messing with him. Except she still had to pay to get the washing machine started. "How much?" She couldn't believe she was reduced to counting quarters. She also wondered how people on tight budgets managed to do their laundry. "Laundry is expensive."

She had to push in the change tray hard. As if the universe was resisting her spending the money.

"Welcome to the real world, Deb."

Great, he was back to calling her Deb. There was a teasing lilt to his voice but still the nickname rankled. However he wasn't wrong. She'd had no idea.

"Your mom did it for you."

She laughed. Her elegant, always perfectly dressed and made-up mother hadn't set foot in a laundry room since she married Tracy's father. Just the thought had her bending over with laughter. "I've never seen my mother do laundry in my life."

He raised a brow.

"The maids did our laundry. I dropped my clothes in a hamper and a few days later they were cleaned, folded or hung up, and put away." She could admit that she was wishing for her parent's household staff right about now. Then she thought about how much she took for granted.

She made a promise to send them thank-you notes. Working on her feet all day had given her a new appreciation for how they had taken care of her family.

"Wow. Must have been nice. My mother worked two jobs, and as the oldest I was in charge of laundry."

"You did the laundry?"

"My dad worked in a restaurant and my mom was always working, it seemed. I was in charge of a lot of stuff. But I mostly tried to pawn the laundry off on my sisters."

"How many sisters do you have?"

"Three."

"Oh my gosh. Any brothers?"

"Two."

"Wow."

"My parents are devout Catholics. They don't believe in birth control." Colt shook his head. "I probably would have more siblings, but they worked a lot."

Tracy's eyes rounded. His house must have been chaotic.

"You?"

She'd grown up in a mansion with her brother and staff. Her parents always seemed to be gone. Either together or separately. There had been more staff in the house than family. And it had been quiet.

"Me and my brother." Concern shimmied down her spine, but she shook it off. Damn Thomas. She needed to talk to him and her family. She wanted her life back. She sighed.

"What now?"

Nothing. But her motel bill was eating into her remaining funds big time. She was already staying at the cheapest place around.

She knew that if she really needed the money, she could find a way to get it. But somehow supporting herself through this strange time had become a point of pride. The allegations of elitism that her father's opponent had leveled at her company had surprised her. Her knee-jerk reaction had been denial but while she was subsisting on a waitress salary and tips she realized that he had a point.

"Wondering how people do this all the time." Her money woes were temporary. She'd be back in Boston soon and this whole crazy financial experiment would be a distant memory. But other people lived this way. Without the safety net she had. She wasn't about to start whining to him. She was curious though. "How long did it take you to adjust to living here?"

"Thinking about making it permanent?"

She thought about the regulars who came in every day or most every day. And the owners and staff of the Speakeasy. Instead of getting frustrated with her, they'd coached her through learning to wait tables.

Chuck and Lottie.

Phoebe and Matteo and Ty and Grace. Alec Rossi and his girlfriend, May Shipley. Griffin Shipley and his wife Audrey. Everyone had been nothing but kind to her.

For a hot moment she thought about what it would be like to

live in a place where people went out of their way to lend a helping hand.

But then she abandoned that thought. Her Fairy Tale Beginnings spin-offs were in Boston. Her career with her father's office was in Boston. Her charity work on the Thayer Family Foundation was in Boston. Her good friends were in Boston. Her life was in Boston.

There was no way she'd end up living in a small town in Vermont permanently. But she would damn well enjoy it while she was here.

Tracy Thayer would sit on the freaking hard plastic chair and make small talk.

But Cee-Cee didn't have to do that. She pushed up and sat on the empty washing machine while he waited for her to mentally work through the answer.

"The idea of living here permanently froze your brain?" But he was smiling.

"No. I can't." Even if being Cee-Cee for the past few days had been wonderful and eye opening. She liked speaking her mind. She liked being part of a crew. She liked the regulars who came into the restaurant.

She even liked *him*. Even as grumpy and cantankerous as he was.

"I'm not one to tell you what you can and can't do." He leaned against the washing machine. They'd eschewed the uncomfortable-looking chairs. "But if you really want something, you should go for it."

She wanted to ask him about his life. But it wasn't polite to bring up scandal. Then she figured screw it. "How did you end up here?"

She wanted to know what happened. How he'd settled in Colebury.

"I saw this waitress at the tractor supply store—"

She nudged him with her shoulder. "I ate at Vega's a few years ago."

"Yeah?"

She waited for him to ask what she thought. But he stayed stubbornly silent.

"Hands down one of the best meals I've ever had."

"Only one of the best?" he teased.

"Do you miss it?"

"No." His answer was abrupt and way too fast. She could push him, but she found she didn't want him to leave.

"Who do you cook for now?"

"No one."

Wait. What? "But you made the soup."

"That was my first time in the kitchen in over a year."

"Do you miss it?"

"Doesn't matter." He made a sharp slashing motion with his hand.

She placed her hand on his arm. His biceps flexed under her fingers. "It does if it upsets you."

He stared at her fingers on his arm and then turned so that her legs straddled his hips. The position change supercharged the atmosphere in the room. The air thickened. Was it hot in here?

Tracy licked her lips and stared into his deep brown eyes, burning with unexpected passion.

"What—" She cleared her throat. "Ah, what are you doing?"

He smirked. "There's a lot of things I haven't done in a year."

Her heart pounded. The attraction that she'd been trying to deny exploded between them. "You looking to break your fast?"

The distraction would be nice. What would Cee-Cee do? She was too nice. She wouldn't take advantage of a guy who clearly needed to work through some things. She'd try to help him work through his issues without taking advantage of him.

This decision was all Tracy.

She trailed her fingers across his bare arms. He shivered in response, his eyes a deep mysterious pool in the warm night air.

His fingers cupped her hips and pulled her closer. Slowly.

Giving her plenty of time to stop what was happening between them. "I am very hungry."

His mouth was a mere inch from hers. The warmth of his minty breath puffed against her lips. Her legs curled around his butt and she leaned toward him.

"Maybe I can help with that." She made the first move, brushing her lips against his mouth. The scruff of his beard tickled her lips and created another level of friction. Her heart pounded.

She kept the kiss light, tentative, testing his response as her eyes drifted closed. His lips clung to hers, with the barest brush of his tongue against her mouth and she opened, inviting him in. Instead, he slid his hands around her neck and held her head in place. His fingers were callused and damaged from his years in the kitchen. But he had a deft and firm touch. Her pulse thudded when he brushed his lips over the throb of her pulse in her neck and along her jaw and behind her ear.

Tracy clung to his biceps, holding on to him as her heart took off.

He tasted each slice of skin as if he were sampling a particularly delicious menu and savoring each bite. Tracy tilted her head back so he could explore to his heart's content.

His skin was warm beneath her fingers as she investigated the veins in his arms and the hard planes of his chest beneath his ever-present Henley.

He tugged her closer so that they were plastered together chest to chest. His fingers slid into her hair at the base of her neck, and shivers raced over her scalp. Her nipples pebbled and she rubbed against his hard muscles.

His erection prodded the soft V of her sex beneath the running shorts she'd put on so she could wash her jeans. She moaned into his mouth as he increased the intensity of the kiss.

He went from tasting to gorging, devouring her one long drugging kiss at a time. Tracy curled her arms around his shoulders and scraped her fingernails through his scalp, his hair a soft silky mass in her hands.

Those clever hands of his drifted over her curves. Tracy moaned at the exponential increase in pressure as he cupped her breasts in his hands and squeezed. He plucked at her with a soft touch that seemed at odds with his gruff exterior. He took his time, in gentle sweeping caresses. The bold, caustic chef had been replaced by an explorer with patience and skill that she hadn't expected.

She'd imagined that he'd be rough and aggressive, a marauder. Instead, he moved with a measured intensity that was all-encompassing.

She nipped at his jaw, encouraging him to take it up a notch. But he continued his slow assault on her senses.

"You're moving way too slow." Her voice came out breathy. She couldn't seem to get enough air. "I like how tight this shirt is."

She yanked the stretchy cotton Henley over his head.

"In the kitchen—" kiss "—you can't have loose clothes." His ran his hands over her shoulders as if he were testing a plump piece of fruit. "They might catch—" kiss "—on something—" kiss "—or catch on fire."

"Too late." Tracy's body had caught on fire. She ran her fingers over his smooth skin, ruffling the light smattering of chest hair.

"It's an easy way to get burned." He plundered her mouth.

A tattoo of a vine with pink roses curled over one shoulder.

She closed her eyes against the dingy backdrop of the dour little laundry room. His touch evoked bright vibrant colors and beams of light.

Her body buzzed with raw awareness. A visceral intensity that she'd never felt before. She liked sex as much as the next girl. But her prior experiences had been tepid compared to this explosion of feelings.

This was a seriously bad idea.

Then again, she was only in town for a few more days. And who better to have a fling with than the hot chef?

Except he was vulnerable. And she was hiding her true identity.

He tugged her to the edge of the washing machine. His cargo shorts couldn't constrain the bulge of his erection. He throbbed against her softer sex; the barrier between them a thin layer.

"This is a terrible idea." He swirled his tongue in the shell of her ear.

He was right. The sense of disappointment was acute. Stronger than she would have expected.

"I don't care," he confessed.

And she was lost.

"Do you?"

She didn't want to lead him on. "I'm not in a place—"

He snorted. "I've been taking life one hour at a time. Believe me, I'm only thinking about how many ways I can make you come."

She moaned, her knees going weak. "Sounds like a plan."

A good plan. A great plan.

He curled his hands beneath her butt and lifted her into his embrace. "Not here."

"Wait." She placed her hand on his chest, her brain sluggish and uncooperative. She kissed him again, slow and deep.

He started walking.

She pulled her mouth from his. "Wait, no."

He stood stock still.

"Not *no*, no."

He nodded slowly. Waiting for her to finish so she got her brain in gear. She gestured over to the box on the wall. "We need condoms."

She could feel the tension leave his body. Another tension invaded.

"Grab the quarters."

This was silly. He could put her down. But the sensation of being cared for caused a slow burn in her belly. She liked it.

They quickly dispensed condoms from the machine and then he carried her to her hotel room. Luckily her cabin was right next door to the entrance to the laundry room in the main building.

No one saw them. But at this point, Tracy didn't care if they did. It would likely be the most excitement Mrs. Beasley had in a decade.

And then she thought, maybe not.

After all, she had installed a condom machine in the laundry room.

That wily old lady.

10

COLT

Colt carried Cee-Cee to her motel room.

On a "bad idea" scale of one to ten this was a fifteen.

But he'd been denying his impulses for over a year. And sex with Cee-Cee wasn't a cigarette or a drink.

When they got to her door, he eased her down carefully.

With a shaking hand, she inserted the key in the lock. She turned the knob slowly as if hesitating.

Colt followed her inside and paused behind her. "You sure about this?"

He would be in pain if he had to walk away.

But he'd get over it.

She turned around quickly. Her normally perfect hair was mussed and tousled around her face. Her mouth was bare of lipstick and swollen with their kisses. Gone was the polished, slightly haughty debutante. In her place was a lush, feminine goddess.

The change in her was striking. He'd had something to do with that transformation. Like when he took a simple vegetable and turned it into a culinary masterpiece. A study of mastery in heat and spice and love.

"Absolutely."

No hesitation.

"*Graças a deus.*" Colt stalked toward her.

She backed to the bed, never taking her gaze from him with a small smirk on her mouth and blue eyes sparkling. There was joy in her lightness and a glow that seemed to surround her like a halo.

Then she stopped retreating and stood still. Meeting him head-on.

He traced her collarbones with a rough finger. She shivered, her nipples hardening in response to the lightest touch. He stared at his darker hand caressing her pale skin. Colt leaned in and pressed a kiss to the sensitive spot behind her ear, inhaling her essence.

"You're a goddess." The goddess of rebirth.

She laughed huskily. "I like the sound of that."

He'd originally dismissed her as wealthy, privileged and spoiled. She was all those things, but she was also human, and kind, with a genuine interest in others.

She was too good for him.

She tilted up her chin and shot him a look. "Talk less."

He laughed.

"Sex more."

"Did you just...."

"Yes, yes, I did."

He placed his hand in the middle of her breastbone and gently pushed her back onto the bed. "I'm not gonna throw away my shot."

He could *Hamilton* with the best of them.

She laughed as she fell down to the mattress, pulling him with her. He landed on top of her body, her legs parting to make way for him.

He liked this version of her. She pushed at the waistband of his shorts, his erection popping out the waistband.

Her soft hands moved over his body, his skin and other things coming alive at her sensual touch as she burrowed beneath his shorts and took him in her hand.

His cock swelled as she pumped him.

Colt tasted her skin that scent of roses and patchouli that was quintessential Cee-Cee invaded his senses, floated around him like a cloud.

He wanted to absorb her essence. To take her in and feast on her goodness. To bask in the way she made him feel.

He made quick work of her clothes, tossing them onto the small chair at the tiny dining table.

He hadn't been this interested in anything in over a year. He wanted to bask in her attention. She scraped her fingernails along his scalp. The sensual move shivered through him.

She kissed him like she was starving.

They dueled with their tongues as she ran her hands over his body. He tasted her with the precision he'd formally reserved only for food. Savoring and lingering over the flavors of her mouth, kissing her eyes, the tip of her nose, the shell of her ear.

But Cee-Cee was having none of it.

She nudged him with her hips and he rolled so that she was on top.

Her small breasts, a perfect handful in his scarred hands, were his for the taking. He sucked a pale pink nipple into his mouth, tonguing the bud, learning what made her squirm and what made her moan.

But she wasn't content to let him have all the fun. She explored with the same passion he did.

He wanted to learn everything about her. To immerse in her essence and her reactions and bring her to new heights. His world tunneled into pleasuring Cee-Cee with a hyper focus he hadn't felt in forever.

But in a surprise move, she took the lead.

She rolled the condom over his erection. He wanted to protest, to slow things down. But he was painfully hard and she was wet and ready for him.

"I don't want to wait." Her breathy plea filled his head.

"Your wish is my command."

She got up on her knees, balancing over him. She was flush with desire, her hair mussed, and her lips swollen. Like a gorgeous nymph, she lowered onto his erection.

His breath caught.

The moment felt...imbued with a certain gravity. And then she seated to the hilt, his cock enveloped by her slick channel, his heart nearly burst in his chest as she began to move over him.

He grasped her butt and pushed up inside her. Cee-Cee closed her eyes, her head thrown back and her mouth open as she climaxed.

Colt couldn't hold back. It had been too long and as her body milked his cock he came with a long groan. His orgasm blasted through him in a rush like steam releasing from a pressure cooker. His heart thundered and he gripped her ass in his hands as he shoved up to kiss her in a hard driving embrace.

Colt's head was spinning.

Cee-Cee was sprawled out over top of him and he was enjoying the sensation of having a sexy woman blanketing him.

His heart thundered, while he recovered slowly from the explosive orgasm. Endorphins and afterglow left him feeling better than he had in a long time. His mouth lifted in a smile. Maybe he'd been approaching his isolation all wrong.

"Do you miss the city?" she asked.

That was a question guaranteed to harsh his mood. But instead of getting upset, he contemplated her question. Absently, he trailed his fingers up and down her spine. Her rose-scented hair tickled his jaw, and her head rested in the curve of his neck.

"Sometimes I miss the pace of it." But he associated that pace and the city with fame and ambition. And that had almost killed him.

"It's kind of nice here though," Cee-Cee murmured softly. "Quiet."

"I can hear myself think here." Introspection was new to him. Back when he'd been working twenty hours a day and chasing accolades, he hadn't had down time. He'd been on the run from the moment he woke until he crashed at night. Always planning the next hill to climb. He'd been so busy climbing that he'd forgotten what the climb was for.

"How did you end up in Colebury?"

"Audrey Shipley is a friend from culinary school. Phoebe too —although I got here first."

"Shipley as in the cider?"

"And the farm and the Busy Bean and half the other businesses in town."

"And you just up and left your life?"

"Initially she offered me a place to hide away and recover."

When Audrey had suggested he come stay out here, at first he'd been reluctant. But it had turned into an excellent decision. Initially he had come to retreat from the world but he'd been out more recently, and he'd begun to reawaken.

"You came here to hide?" There was an odd note in her voice.

"Yeah." Colt played with the ends of her hair. "I needed to get away from the press. Get away from the destructive behaviors that led me to have a complete meltdown." He knew she knew his backstory and what had happened.

But when she nodded there was a tightness in her body that wasn't there before.

"That quest for fame is what destroyed me." Colt could talk about it now without wanting to flee. He'd a lot of time to think about what he wanted…and what he didn't want out of life. "I had formed destructive patterns that put me and my family in jeopardy. I am never going back to that lifestyle."

She lay very still as if his words wounded her in some elemental way. "I completely understand your position."

His position? It wasn't like he was writing a paper on the evils of fame. "I can think of better positions to discuss." She'd been on top the first time. She'd taken the lead and he'd loved her assertiveness. But now it was time to mix things up.

"Oh yeah?"

Colt rolled so she lay beneath him. "Let's start with this one next," he whispered in her ear. "I think you'll find it very satisfying."

"I'll need more research to determine if your hypothesis is accurate." The smile was back on her face. That momentary still-ness had been obliterated by her sunny demeanor.

"Research is my second-favorite pastime." Colt kissed his way down her body.

"What's your first?" There was a curiosity and teasing light-ness in her voice.

"This." And he proceeded to show her.

TRACY

Tracy rolled out of bed the next morning.

Colt had spent the night. He lay on his stomach in the bed, the sheets draped over his legs and the curve of his very spectacular ass, one hairy leg sticking out of the covers, and his arms hugging the pillow like he'd wrapped around her last night.

Just like her fantasy from the other day. And the reality was even more phenomenal than that brief daydream.

Last night had been amazing.

Beyond amazing. She really, really wanted to talk to her friend Courtney Lee right now. She needed her advice and counsel. Although Court had her own problems. She'd been in love with their friend Jay for years. They'd been sneaking around, never acknowledging the relationship in public, thinking no one knew. Courtney was on the cusp of breaking it off. At least Tracy thought. So she definitely wasn't the queen of healthy relationships but she would understand Tracy's dilemma.

Since they met, Colt had been a challenging presence in her daily life. There was an ease between them that she had never found with a lover or even many of her friends.

She was always hiding things.

But when he'd admitted to destructive patterns, she remembered the article she'd read about him. He never drank alcohol now even though he'd been spending a decent amount of time in the gastropub. And he'd admitted he'd given up smoking. Maybe those tabloid rumors had been accurate.

A sudden despair overcame her.

If he knew who she was, if he knew what kind of scrutiny his connection to her—and by association, her family—would bring upon him, he'd run screaming from the bed, from her life. But, she really liked him.

He'd taken time out of his day to help her with laundry. Although since he was in bed with her maybe that wasn't all altruistic. But he'd helped out Phoebe when she'd had a conflict. He'd met with Chuck and Lottie and been an active participant in discussing their menu for their fiftieth anniversary. He'd pushed past an understandable reluctance to get involved because someone else needed his help.

He was a good person.

His fall from grace clearly hadn't crushed his giving spirit.

His gruff, sometimes abrasive manner hid a generous and kind soul.

The last thing he needed was to be connected to Tracy Thayer. The press and her family would eviscerate him. They would chew him up and spit him out. Dredging up all the hurts and negative news from his past and making him relive it all over again.

She would not allow his association with her and her family to wound his spirit.

Good thing this was just a fling.

Her heart faltered because even though she believed it when she'd told him that she wasn't looking for anything permanent or lasting, somewhere deep the recesses of her thirteen-year-old heart, there lived a hope that she would find her fairy tale.

Someone who loved her in spite of the problems her family would bring to a relationship. Someone who she could be completely honest with and who would share their burdens with her too. Not just their burdens but their joy.

But that really was a dream. She couldn't tell him, couldn't tell anyone about her family's secrets. And she liked him too much to allow him to be hurt because she wanted a lover who would support her.

She needed to shove him out of her bed and out of her heart.

Good thing he was averse to starting a relationship.

"You're thinking awfully hard over there." His voice rumbled from the smushed recesses of the pillow.

"Yes," she said regretfully.

His impressive butt muscles flexed as he rolled over. He lazily skimmed his gaze over her naked body, and his cock began to harden. "Somehow I don't think it's about what to get for breakfast."

Before she could deny she was hungry, her stomach rumbled in response.

"Personally, I'm thinking about a different kind of sustenance," he teased.

He tugged her back to bed and she let him pull her back down to the rough cotton sheets.

His cock jutted between them as he trailed his fingers over the curve of her waist. Her skin pebbled in response. He had working hands so different from her softer ones. But his touch was tender and erotic and lit her up like the Boston Harbor on the Fourth of July.

Even though she knew she was bad for him, that being in a relationship would be detrimental to his health and happiness, she let him pull her back to bed. There would be time to disentangle and leave him alone.

No one was here in this room now but the two of them. Together they created an incendiary heat that she couldn't ignore.

A few hours later, she was still with Colt.

She'd woken up the second time to the realization that her clothes were still in the washing machine. She pulled his Henley over her head, easier than her iron maiden sports bra, and grabbed her running shorts. She headed to the laundry room. Luckily no one else had been in here so she was able to dump everything in one dryer. She studied the dials with the concentration of a doctor about to perform brain surgery.

He'd followed her wearing only his shorts, and the view was amazing. He had flat abs and sculpted shoulders with that rose vine tattoo climbing over his skin. Reminding her that the sex had been amazing.

"Just put everything on low. You can't go wrong with that." Colt was amused.

She'd been subtly trying to get rid of him. Of course, maybe she was sending mixed messages because she'd stolen his shirt. She didn't want him to leave. She was bad for him. But she wanted him.

Her stomach rumbled even louder.

"Let's get some food." Colt cajoled her.

"I can't go out like this." She hadn't taken a shower. Her makeup was gone, burned off by a marathon of sex. Her hair was probably a complete nest. "My mother would have a heart attack."

He raised a brow. "Is your mother here?"

She loved that he didn't question the fact that she still listened to her mother. Sort of. Family was important to him. Tracy and her mother's relationship had been strained for years but she still followed directions and toed the family line. And she loved her mother, even if she didn't understand her choices.

She flushed. "I need to take a shower first." She did have a pair of linen pants and a silk short-sleeve shirt she could wear. Or the running shorts and sports bra.

Maybe he'd grow impatient with her stalling and leave. Then she wouldn't have to kick him out.

"Just throw on a hat," he said.

She only had her wide-brimmed beach hat in the rental. And it wouldn't go with her more casual workout clothes.

He eyed her hair. "I have a baseball cap you can borrow."

Tracy winced. A baseball cap? Even when she attended Red Sox games, she didn't wear a ball cap.

Before she could decline, he asked, "What's really going on?"

"I don't think I'm good for you," Tracy replied miserably. Actually she knew she wasn't. But kicking him out and cutting him loose when he'd been the bright spot in her days was incredibly hard.

"I think you were very, very bad for me." He grinned, his teeth white in the sexy, joyful curve of his mouth.

She snorted. But she was struck in this moment at how much younger he looked. How much freer he seemed. Had she done that?

She was tempted by the idea that she had impacted him. That thought filled her with immense satisfaction.

"It's just breakfast. Not a lifetime commitment." He threaded his fingers through hers so casually.

It was just breakfast.

And she wanted to spend just a little more time with him before she returned to her lonely life. She was in a holding pattern as far as research regarding the app and Esme. She was off at the Speakeasy today.

"What's your favorite breakfast?" He asked the question out of the blue.

"Umm." She normally had a cup of coffee and a protein bar. She wouldn't say it was a favorite.

"Wait. You don't have a favorite?" He looked appalled. "I am seriously offended."

"I don't really think that much about food."

"I don't even know how to address that." Colt looked at her as if she'd just admitted to being a serial killer. "I make—" He paused, swallowed. "Made a divine veggie hash with poached eggs in a cradle of diced root vegetables and black beans with the subtlest hint of smoked paprika and coriander."

She couldn't interpret the look on his face. Maybe a hint of longing.

That actually sounded pretty good—similar to the Breakfast for Dinner dish served at the Speakeasy.

"It's a great way to start the day," Colt said quietly.

"Coffee is my breakfast of choice."

He assessed her for a moment, then shook his head. "Coffee."

As far as she knew, the only breakfast-y place was the diner. But she guaranteed their coffee wasn't strong enough for her. The Gin Mill and the Speakeasy only served lunch and dinner. The Busy Bean was more coffee shop with pastries. As a matter of fact, the menu was…problematic for her. But the coffee was fabulous. "We can go to the Bean."

"Look at you being all local. Audrey makes some amazing pastries."

Once her clothes were dry, Tracy retrieved her laundry from the dryer and dumped it on the motel bed. She put on her running shorts and a clean tank top and her work shoes. She shuddered. Good thing no one she knew could see her.

Colt led her to his truck. A beat-up old Chevy Silverado. The passenger door didn't lock and the driver's seat had a worn bowl from being used so much.

He drove to the Busy Bean. They really did have the best coffee.

At the last minute, she grabbed his ball cap from the back seat.

The patrons of the coffee shop looked up when the bell over the door tinkled and they walked in.

Normally, people looked up when the door opened, probably to see if it was someone they knew, and then retreated to their conversation once they realized she was no one of importance. But this morning, it was like she could feel the speculation swirl around the room. But was it because of Colt? Hopefully yes.

While they waited in line to order their drinks, she started to worry. She didn't think anyone was looking at her. But what if somehow, someone here recognized her? She felt raw, exposed.

Crap. She should have thought ahead.

In the Speakeasy, customers tended to ignore their waitstaff. In the past, she'd been guilty of the same thing—not really noting any personal characteristics of the person waiting on her unless she needed something from them. She was always polite. A Thayer never made a scene.

But she couldn't say that she'd ever considered her servers as more than someone there to wait on her.

The rhetoric in the news had ramped up. Her father's opponent in the upcoming election continued to keep the story alive and roiling with his claims of elitism and a politician out of touch with the regular guy. She'd hoped that the news would cycle to some new scandal but so far that hadn't happened.

Poor Yolanda was fielding all the business phone calls. The press had also been clamoring at her for an interview. So far the company had only put out a couple of statements, standing behind the integrity of their process and pointing to all the matches that they had facilitated over the past year. Tracy was going to have to give her a big raise.

"What's up?"

He could sense her discomfort. Had anyone ever been as attuned to her as he was? She didn't think so.

"It's pretty crowded in here." Tracy shifted closer to him.

A woman in a chair at the corner of the shop seemed to be surveying everyone with a speculative eye. But then the bell over the door rang and the woman waved at the young couple who came in.

Tracy relaxed. She was glad she'd put on Colt's John Deere cap. The two-toned white mesh and feathered green hat with the suede patch didn't match her running shorts and yoga top, but it concealed her face. Tracy Thayer would never be caught dead in a ratty old ball cap. But Cee-Cee rather enjoyed it.

"You want to get it to go and eat somewhere else?" Colt asked.

"Where?"

"Give me suggestions."

They could go back to her motel room, but Mrs. Beasley needed time to clean it. And she couldn't guarantee that if she were back in that room that she wouldn't jump him one more time.

"Somewhere away." If she was going to enjoy this time with him, she wanted to be away from everything where the real world couldn't intrude.

He nodded.

She studied the specials board and found something she could eat. She ordered the cup of oatmeal with brown sugar and pecans while Colt ordered a biscuit with bacon and cheddar that sounded amazing. Except for all that gluten.

Ten minutes later they were back in his truck. The tension that gripped her eased now that they were secluded in the intimacy of the front seat of his truck.

"You want to come to my place?"

His place? She was curious to see where he lived. He was a classically trained chef, he'd been to Paris, he'd worked in New York and Boston. What things did he surrounded himself with? What clues could she unearth that would reveal more of his personality?

She shouldn't spend more time with him, but she couldn't

seem to stop. "Sure. It beats the Three Bears. Pretty sure Mrs. Beasley is looking out for a glimpse of your bare ass."

Of course it was a spectacular ass, so Tracy really couldn't blame her.

COLT

Colt pulled into his grass driveway, following in the worn tire tracks, and drove toward his cabin. He was unexpectedly nervous. The slant roof, single-room cabin had a porch that ran the length of the small structure.

She'd tried to cut him loose this morning. Some bullshit about not being good for him. But she clearly believed it.

She might just be the best thing that had happened to him in months. He had laughed more in the past few days than he had for the entire past year. She'd made him forget his own troubles. The last time he remembered feeling this way, wanting to just spend time in a place, was when he had opened his first restaurant and he'd spent hours there alone. Absorbing the atmosphere and soaking up every detail about the space and how he felt. He'd never felt this way about a woman, about any person really, and he wanted to spend more time in her company.

To see if it was just a fluke or if there was something more there.

"Bring your breakfast up to the porch and I'll get some plates."

"I can just eat from the—"

He shot her a look. "Food is a sensual experience. It starts with your eyes." Just because they got takeout didn't mean they should treat the food as disposable. She followed him up onto the porch and he gestured to the rockers. "Have a seat and I'll be right out."

Meals were meant to be savored. In a metal gardener's basket, he carried out the table settings: heavy lapis Fiestaware plates and a bowl for her breakfast, bright yellow hand-thrown coffee mugs he'd picked up at a booth at the Colebury Farmers Market one day when his friends dragged him out of his reclusive existence, and cloth napkins and silverware.

He gestured for her bag. She handed it over and he fished out her cup of oatmeal. He grimaced. All those excellent baked goods and she'd gone for the most bland, albeit healthy, item on the menu.

He scooped the oatmeal into the bowl and placed her bowl on the cloth napkin, pale blue with buzzing yellow bees, then set the combo on top of the blue plate. He set the plate on the mini bistro table. He pulled a pair of shears from the gardening basket near the front door and loped down to the edge of the woods to snip some flowers. The cluster of daisies in purples and whites drooped with a goofy cheer.

She sat in quiet bemusement as he plated their breakfast, poured their coffee into the ceramic mugs, and settled the daisies into a creamy milk-glass vase.

"This is so gorgeous." She pulled out her phone. "Can I take a picture—only of the food," she clarified. "I'll tag the Busy Bean and the town. You can never have too much good publicity."

He frowned at the phone. "Have you thought about just enjoying the moment?"

"That's difficult for me." She snapped a few pictures and then tucked the phone away. "I don't have time for enjoyment."

"You should make time." Of course he couldn't really judge. Until his forced retirement, he'd worked twenty hours a day and was always chasing the next accolade. He hadn't relaxed for years.

"I've got a lot of…responsibilities." She shrugged, seeming far away and somewhat sad. "In theory, all publicity is good publicity."

He just shook his head. "Not in my world."

"Good point."

They ate their breakfast in silence. The song of the crickets and birds were background music. The air was thick with the scents of roses and honeysuckle. His biscuit was really good. He'd chosen one with bacon, cheddar and green onion.

The sun rose higher in the sky, bathing his garden in a brilliant light, highlighting the textures and the colors. The plot had grown over the summer. While he'd always understood the relationship between methods for growing food and preparing delicious meals, he hadn't ever had his own garden. His mom had a small one when they'd been kids.

They talked idly about the weather and the sunshine and the fact that his vegetable plants were lush with produce: The pale orange zucchini blossoms, the bright red cherry tomatoes, the thick green cucumbers, and the multi-colored bell peppers.

That would make a really excellent salad with a warm bacon dressing and crumbles of local Vermont blue cheese.

He was lost in composing the recipe when she took out her phone and snapped some more pictures of his garden.

"I've got a challenge for you." Colt shoved down the hit of annoyance. He didn't have any right to be irritated with her. They were just hanging out enjoying a quiet summer morning. But he thought she needed the break more than he did.

"Sure."

"Put your phone away for an hour."

The look on her face should have been a huge red flag.

"You can't do it." He would take it as a personal challenge to get her to forsake her phone.

"Of course I can." She hesitated. "But what are we going to do?"

The uncertainty of her reaction spurred him on. They could go inside and have more sex. He certainly wouldn't turn that down. But he found himself wanting to play.

"Apple picking."

"Apple picking?" she said slowly.

"Yup."

"I haven't been apple picking since college."

"It's a little early but the Paula Reds and the Ginger Gold trees should have some ripe fruit by now." He rubbed his hands together. "They'd be perfect for a cobbler maybe with a little cheddar and a drizzle of Lyon honey over the topping."

He pulled up. He'd been composing the dish in his head and mentally going through the necessary steps to prepare it. Visualization. He hadn't even hesitated.

A weird unsettled feeling stole his breath. This wasn't like the soup where he'd been coerced into helping Phoebe. This was him, creating a dish, and actively thinking about cooking.

Just like with the salad a few minutes ago.

"You're going to bake a cobbler?" The pleasure in her voice was hard to miss. She smiled ruefully. "Too bad I can't eat it."

What? "You need to worry less about your weight. Life is meant to be lived, a banquet of tastes and textures and experiences."

"I have celiac disease. I can't have gluten unless you want me in your bathroom for the next twenty-four hours." She clapped a hand over her mouth as if appalled by what she'd just said.

Celiac. So not just avoiding carbs but actively sick from the gluten in flour. The protein damaged the small intestine. He'd made assumptions without getting enough information. "I'm sorry I misjudged you."

"Not a big deal." She smiled. "I do pay attention to what I eat so it was a logical conclusion. It was just incorrect."

Her smile washed away his remorse.

His brain whirled with so many thoughts. He'd judged her the other day in the Speakeasy. He should know better. But one thought stood out. He was determined to make something she could eat. Considering and discarding different grain options while his brain worked out the cooking problem.

She sighed. "I really do miss baked goods. My nanny used to make the most wonderful cinnamon rolls that I loved. Haven't had them in so long I've forgotten what they taste like."

"I'll come up with something you can eat."

"Oh." Her face glowed with pleasure. "That would be...wonderful."

Maybe a fruit galette with buckwheat flour? Or a savory *Pão de Queijo* with tapioca flour?

He wasn't-well versed in all the different options for gluten-free cooking. He'd always just arrogantly used what he wanted and screw the customer. But now he found himself wanting to please her.

11

TRACY

Tracy was halfway up a tree carefully picking apples from an ancient tree.

The ladder had been just standing in the middle of a row in between the trees. Off to their left, some newer tree varieties with clusters of unripe fruit had been trained to grow flat on espaliers to maximize the available space. Bees buzzed in the warm late summer air searching for pollen, and birds chirped and sang songs flitting between the trees.

Each section of the orchard had their own variety. The beginning of a section of trees was marked with a fancy wood plaque, engraved with wood burning script, stating the type of apple and when the trees had been planted.

According to Colt different apples were good for different food because of sweetness, texture, and moisture content. Who knew?

Colt wore a bandana over his hair, his skin bronzed from the day in the sun.

His T-shirt read Choose Your Weapon with a row of kitchen utensils, only two of which Tracy recognized, the whisk and the knife. He'd cut the sleeves off the shirt, his bare arms showing off his biceps.

He'd found bicycles in the shed behind the tiny cabin and they'd biked along the tire tracks and into the neighboring orchard. When he'd lifted her onto the bike, she had to wonder why they hadn't just gone back to bed.

Bed was nice. Lots of sex. Lots of intimacy.

Instead she was up a ladder, getting hit in the face with leaves while she reached through branches, straining to grab an apple.

"Going to the grocery store would be a lot easier," she teasingly grumped.

"But this is more fun."

"Your idea of fun is different than mine." But she was kidding.

He was next to her as she strained on her toes to grab a beautiful red apple that was slightly out of reach. "Let me get it." He easily plucked the apple, his arm brushing hers. "That's a gorgeous apple."

He rubbed the fruit on his T-shirt until it was shiny, then took a giant bite. The crunch was loud as he bit into the apple. He was smiling as he did it. Smiling!

"Yum." He finished chewing and then held it out to her. "Have a bite."

Tracy grabbed his wrist with one hand and held on. She leaned forward, her gaze not leaving his as she took a bite of his apple. She chewed the sweet and tart treat slowly, savoring the fresh fruit.

When she was finished with her bite, she said, "I thought Eve gave Adam the apple."

"You want to sin with me?" Colt raised his eyebrow.

"I thought we already did."

"Practice makes perfect," Colt shot back.

She laughed. She thought about how much fun they'd had in bed. She'd been able to let loose and be herself. "Anytime, Chef Man."

Colt studied the apple in his hand. "It's believed that the fruit wasn't really an apple. That it was a pomegranate." He got a faraway look in his eyes. "I make a summer salad with arugula, pomegranate, goat cheese, and pulled pork with a ras el hanout spice rub that is out of this world."

"That sounds amazing." She loved that he'd said I *make*, present tense, not I *made*, past tense as if he wouldn't again. "What is ras el hanout?" She wanted to keep him talking about food. His face was pure joy when he was discussing cooking. He missed it. That was clear from the way he talked about it. But she knew better than to push him into cooking.

"It's a mix of spices—cinnamon, cardamom, cumin, paprika, clove, nutmeg, allspice, coriander, ginger, turmeric chili peppers— used in North African/Middle Eastern/Moroccan cooking. I make my own blend but it varies depending on what I can find."

"Yum." She knew better than to push but she really hoped she got a chance to taste that dish. To distract him, she said, "I make a mean microwaved leftover of barbeque takeout."

"It really is appalling that you don't know how to cook."

She could make excuses, but the truth was she hadn't had time or the interest to learn. "Why learn when there are all these amazing chefs out there ready to ply me with their creations?"

"Ply you?" He laughed as he helped her down the ladder. "You really are a princess."

"I don't have a crown charm for nothing." She shook her bracelet at him.

They wandered through the orchard, the scent of sweet sap and flowers in the air. Bees swooped and buzzed in a lazy arch through the bright blue sky. Puffy white clouds floated like marshmallow fluff.

"Look at those clouds." Colt had stopped and was staring up at the sky. "Like a perfect Pavlova."

"Oh, I had one at Café Boulud in New York." The sweet treat had dissolved on her tongue.

"What do you see?" he prodded.

She looked around. "Trees."

"In the sky." Silly.

"Not much. It hurts my neck."

"Then lie down."

"On the ground?"

"Absolutely. We can watch the clouds go by."

He plopped on the ground and lay back, beckoning to her. Tracy studied the ground, studied him, noting the free and easy smile on his face. She didn't want that happy, carefree look to disappear, so she dropped down next to him.

"Didn't you do this as a kid?" Colt said from beside her.

"Get my clothes dirty and my hair mussed?" She shuddered. "Not unless I wanted to get yelled at."

"Okay. I promise not to yell at you if your hair is messy," he teased. "Lie back."

"And do what?"

"Just stare at the clouds. Watch the world go by. Dream. Do nothing."

That sounded both incredibly simple and incredibly hard all at the same time.

Do nothing? Thayers were never idle. There were always new people to meet and causes to champion.

She lay beside him, stiff and a little weirded out that she was literally lying in dirt and grass.

"Try to relax."

"It's harder than you'd think."

"I was there once." Colt threaded his fingers with hers. They lay side by side, their arms touching, his toes touching hers, partially shaded by the canopy of the largest apple tree but still able to see the sky. "But now I try to take in simpler pleasures."

She tried to relax. She loved listening to his voice, the nuances and the subtle emotions when he talked about experiencing life. She'd never met anyone as determined to just be present in his life without the push to always be doing more. It was incredibly appealing.

"Are you happy?" She was truly curious. After all, at one time he'd been running a restaurant empire.

He didn't toss off a flip answer. He hesitated, as if he were really thinking about her question. "Not yet. But I'm getting there. Look, that one looks like a giant honey pot."

She didn't see it. "I think that one looks like Lincoln's top hat." She pointed to another one.

"Did you know when he was a lawyer he used to keep his papers inside the hat?"

She laughed. "That's an interesting thing to know."

"I had an excellent grade school history teacher."

They lay on their backs pointing at the clouds and saying what they thought each cloud looked like. Their answers were wildly divergent, but their amusement was joint.

After a few more minutes, they got up and finished filling their baskets with fruit.

Tracy could feel the slight warmth over her nose and cheeks.

Getting outside had been the right call.

Her heart was pumping from the exercise and full of gratitude for the beautiful day as they biked back with a basket overflowing with apples, sailing along the dirt tracks to Colt's cabin. Where he might cook for her.

He'd looked so shocked when he was talking about making the cobbler. Getting back into the kitchen again of his own accord was a big step.

They made it back to the cabin without mishap even though it had been a long time since she'd been on a bike. She dropped the kickstand and grabbed her BPA-free water bottle, quenching her thirst from the sun and the exercise.

She couldn't remember the last time she'd felt so free. She dropped the bottle and held out her arms, then whirled around with her head tilted toward the bright blue sky.

"What are you doing?" He was laughing.

"Making myself dizzy." She stopped spinning and teetered in front of him. Her head continued to whirl, the sensation making her feel light and free. Tracy took one step and lurched to the right.

Luckily Colt was there to catch her. "Whoa."

She laughed. "You caught me."

"I did," he said softly.

"Don't drop the apples." He had the basket looped over his forearm. The weight of the fruit flexed his muscles. She couldn't say that she'd ever really considered arms sexy but when she studied his, she decided that they were totally sexy. "You have sexy forearms."

He flushed. "That's not a thing."

"Sure it is." Tracy said slyly, "I'm looking right at them. And they are seeexxxx-eee. Total arm porn."

He snorted. "If I didn't know better, I'd think you were drunk."

"Ha-ha." Tracy spun around again. Cee-Cee was feeling frisky and irreverent. "Drunk on life!" she shouted.

As they headed toward the charming porch of the cabin, she realized she hadn't reached for her phone in the past hour.

Instead she reached for his hand. His palm was solid against hers and she swung their arms.

"You twirl around like that often?" he asked curiously.

"Nope. I never really had time to be a kid." She'd been expected to be present regularly, especially during election years. Her parents trotted out the perfect family, the fairy-tale romance, the obedient and accomplished children. She was considered well rounded, she played the piano, had a mean doubles game, could tack a sailboat, and converse on world politics. She wasn't sure when she'd started to hate the expectations but she had definitely soured over the past few years.

She and her brother were very different. He'd loved the media attention. She'd learned to use it to her advantage, but she'd never enjoyed the need to always be on for the camera and the press and the voters.

Fortunately, nowadays she was mainly in the background.

Until all this hoopla with her matchmaking app. Normally, she worked in her father's Boston office part-time. Worked at their family foundation part-time. And monitored her Fairy Tale business daily.

His look was quizzical.

"There were always obligations," she shared reluctantly. Dinners, parties, photo ops. "My family was very active socially."

Colt shuddered.

"It wasn't all bad. I liked dressing up. And I loved meeting new people. Everyone is so different."

There had been good times. There'd also been plenty of times when she'd had to smile and pretend when inside her heart was breaking. Every fucking time someone brought up her parent's marriage and their fairy-tale romance, the wealthy young scion who met and married a woman from a totally different background and how deliriously happy they seemed, she'd wanted to throw up. That part she had loved until she found out that the media story that her father and mother perpetuated was a lie and that her parents had been unfaithful for years.

"So far you aren't convincing me."

"I love learning about people's stories. Where they came from. Where they are going. What they want out of life." Finding ways to connect them. She shook off the memories. "What was growing up like at your house?"

"Fairly typical. My dad worked in a friend's small restaurant. My mom was an office manager during the day and she helped at the restaurant at night. It was loud, chaotic, happy."

"You got along with your siblings?"

"Sure. I mean we fought over dumb stuff, of course. And mornings before school with three sisters was a nightmare."

"A nightmare?"

"One of my sisters was really into makeup and fashion. We had two bathrooms for the eight of us." He had a reminiscent smile on his face. "Man, she used to have cosmetic shit all over the place. Creams, and brushes, and tubes of color. And God forbid if we touched it. Or used it. That was cause for death."

Sisters and brothers and chaos. It sounded like fun. And so different from her very proper, very quiet upbringing. "Sounds lovely."

"I used to dream about living alone." He had stared into the distance. "I still remember thinking that I would have made it if I had my own place. But when I finally got my own fancy apartment in the North End, I was never there to enjoy it. You'd think that after the chaos of the restaurant and the dance of working in a fully functioning busy kitchen that that quiet would be nice... but it was so quiet."

"Too quiet?"

"Maybe." Colt shrugged. "I was never home. And at the end I was usually drunk."

Oh. He was sharing, admitting that he'd had a problem. "You live alone now."

"True." Colt nodded.

It was invasive and none of her business. Tracy Thayer would never in a million years ask so personal a question, but Cee-Cee didn't have a filter. "You still drinking?"

"Gave it up." Colt looked her straight in the eye, his gaze serious, intent. "I had to. It was killing me. It was all killing me. I will never go back to that life in the spotlight. It's toxic."

His words struck like a knife to the heart. Today had been lovely. Every moment imbued with a beauty and serenity that had been missing in her life for far too long.

But with that sentence she knew it was time. "I should go."

COLT

Colt had screwed up.

Today had been one of the best in recent memory. Last night's sex had been amazing, The physical intimacy was easy to brush away. Maybe it was because it had been a while. Over a year. But he didn't think so.

Before, he'd been so mired in his own head that sex hadn't even been on his radar.

But last night had been fun and healing and right now he was feeling great.

Today had been a different kind of intimacy. The sheer wholesomeness of it. He felt as if he'd been living shrouded in mist and suddenly the fog had cleared and the sun had come out. That was all Cee-Cee.

But something he'd said had upset her.

He'd have to be blind to miss when her smile dimmed, and she abruptly decided to leave. He had wanted to argue. To cajole. But maybe she was right to head back to her motel.

This connection between them was temporary. She didn't live here. She had a life somewhere else.

And he had no intention of leaving. He'd found a measure of peace in the country that he had no desire to give up.

He wasn't about to upset that balance.

A few hours later, Colt was still thinking about her. He'd dropped her off at the motel. She hadn't invited him in. Which was fine.

Instead his brain had gone to their conversation this morning.

He'd stopped by the Kwik Stop on the way home and to his surprise he found a section of Bob's Red Mill products, including gluten-free flours.

He had a basket full of apples and visions of different ideas dancing in his head. His palms itched with the desire to get back in the kitchen. He'd bought the flours and other cooking supplies…just in case.

When he got back to the cabin, he put the baking goods away and pretended they didn't exist.

The next morning, after weeding the garden and then trying to spend a few hours editing his current freelance project, he gave up.

His head and heart continued to wander and be distracted by the thoughts of flavors and textures dancing in his brain. Finally, he gave in to the longing to get back in the kitchen.

He stood in the tiny kitchen of his cabin.

There was a window over the sink flanked by upper cabinets that held the dishes and some pantry basics. He had no idea what supplies he had. He wasn't even sure he had a cutting board. He didn't cook. He scrambled the occasional egg and ate sandwiches and salads. That was it.

Prior to making the soup the other day, just looking at a knife caused him to start shaking.

He rooted around in the silverware drawer and way in the back behind the caddy that held the cutlery he found a small paring knife. The blade was dull. He'd have better luck using a spoon than trying to cut a thing with this knife. He found a stone in the small yard that he thought would work as a whetstone for sharpening the knife. He drew the blade along the stone, the long slow strokes soothing him.

After sharpening the knife, he began to peel the apples. He sliced apples until he had a good pile. He needed a mix of the two for what he'd planned.

He set up his *mise en place*, lining up the ingredients along the counter like little soldiers. Digging through the pantry, he found cinnamon, cardamom, and nutmeg.

He didn't have any baking tins, so he grabbed the cast iron skillet he'd been using to fry his eggs in the morning.

An hour later, his cabin was filled with the aroma of fall. Warm spices and baking apples filled the air as the first dish he'd created in over a year baked in the oven. Colt cleaned up the kitchen, absently applying the sanitation tasks and cleanup protocol. The actions rote like riding a bicycle—he didn't even have to think about them.

He'd cooked—and nothing bad had happened. He hadn't

even thought about searching the pantry for a bottle. He'd taken pleasure in the repetitive movement of using the knife and creating uniform slices for the filling.

He'd used his hands to knead the mixture for the topping.

He pulled the bubbling treat from the oven. The crust was a deep golden brown. His mouth watered at the nutty aroma of the buckwheat and the oats. And all he could think was that he wanted to share it with her.

He reached for his cell to call her. And realized he had no idea what her phone number was. But he did know where she "lived."

Once the dessert was cool enough, he wrapped the skillet in a cotton dish towel with pumpkins and leaves on it. Without stopping to consider the wisdom of showing up unannounced, he hopped in his truck and sped toward the Three Bears Motor Lodge.

When he arrived, he hesitated. Maybe this was too stalkerish.

She'd tell him to leave if she didn't want some cobbler. Or he could offer to drop it off and go.

He didn't want to equate a refusal of the food with a refusal of him, but the thought lingered in his brain. If she didn't want the cobbler, it didn't mean that she didn't want him. And he would get over it if she didn't want him.

Before he could talk himself out of it, Colt headed for her motel cabin. He knocked on the door cautiously.

The parking lot was full of plumbing trucks.

The door swung wide and he was presented with her back as she called over her shoulder. "I'm almost done. I'll be out of your hair as soon as I can."

There was a panicky note to her voice. But Colt was struck by the pile of clothes on the bed and the open suitcase. "You're leaving?"

His heart crumpled.

She didn't owe him anything so he wasn't sure why her potential absence stabbed his at his tender feelings. He didn't think she was ready to commit to marriage or anything but a heads-up that she was bugging out would have been nice.

She whirled around. "Colt!"

Instead of the reaction he expected, for her to be annoyed that he had shown up unannounced, she rushed over to him and threw her arms around him. He grunted and held on to the cast iron pan, barely.

"What's wrong?"

But relief cascaded through him. She wasn't leaving *him*.

TRACY

Tracy wrapped her arms around him and squeezed. Just for a minute.

She was ridiculously pleased to see him. She was embarrassed to admit that in the past when she had an issue with her living space, she called a manager or an assistant to deal with the problem with as little inconvenience to her as possible. Once the call was made, someone else took care of the problem.

None of this was Mrs. Beasley's fault. But for a few frustrated minutes she felt trapped.

She only had a few hundred dollars left and the hotel rooms in Burlington were much more expensive than Colebury. She wondered again how regular people navigated life.

She had been doing just fine, being careful with her remaining money, but there was no room in her miniscule budget for this unexpected expense.

The truth was she could go home at any time.

Bernie, her father, even the press couldn't stop her.

But somewhere along the way, surviving without her family had become a point of pride. And she had developed an appreciation and understanding for why her father's opponent had criticized Fairy Tale Beginnings. She really had not understood how out of reach that registration fee was for so many people.

Colt awkwardly circled her shoulders and squeezed. She had been thrilled to see him. Just for a moment someone else to commiserate and share her burdens and worries.

"What's wrong?"

"There's a plumbing problem and Mrs. Beasley doesn't have any available rooms." It was a little weird, but Mrs. Beasley had been very intent when she'd explained that Tracy needed to leave.

She'd also dropped the bomb that some reporters had checked in to the other rooms.

Mrs. Beasley made it a point to tell Tracy that they were overflow for an event in Burlington. She'd put her wrinkled hand on Tracy's forearm and spoken quietly. As if she knew that reporters would be bad for her. But she hadn't ever given any indication that she knew who Tracy was.

Reporters!

They weren't here for her. But it would definitely be better if she weren't around.

"So where are you going?" His voice rumbled through his chest beneath her ear.

"I haven't figured that out." She glanced at her little leather backpack. Thinking about her remaining cash. "It's going to be more...challenging to get to work if I'm staying in Burlington." She squared her shoulders. "But I can make it work. Hopefully it's just for a day or so."

"Stay with me," he blurted out.

She jerked back. "What?"

He cleared his throat. "You're welcome to stay with me."

But...they barely knew each other. One night of spectacular sex and sharing childhood memories barely made a dent in the volumes of things they didn't know about each other.

"You would...do that for me?"

"You won't be too far from the Speakeasy and you can save money if you don't need to pay for your room," Colt continued.

"Or if it makes you feel better, you can pay me a rental fee. But I don't want or need your money."

Tracy mulled over the idea.

It seemed an imprudent choice. Share a small cabin with her crush. After all, she would be leaving soon, and he would hate her family dynamic and the press's interest in her family and life if he ever discovered it.

However, she would definitely be off the grid. No way reporters could track her to his tiny cabin.

The truth was…she liked him.

She liked him a lot. He'd survived a crushing blow and he was working toward peace. She respected him and his efforts to get better. To be better.

"I shouldn't." She headed for her suitcase. She had to finish packing because the repair people needed to get in her room. And she needed to get out of here.

"You should." He shoved a skillet at her. "I made an apple cobbler with our pickings."

She smiled, her heart expanding. "You cooked! That's great."

"I made this for you."

"I can't—"

"It's gluten-free."

She paused while folding a Speakeasy T-shirt and peered at the treat. So much to unpack in this moment. She inhaled deeply. It smelled heavenly. Like sugar and cinnamon and spice and all the things that seemed like they would go with a cozy family home.

So very different from the mansion she'd grown up in.

He was offering her a chance to experience that feeling of a home. Of that emotional intimacy that she'd believed out of her reach.

"You cooked," she said again softly.

"I couldn't get the recipe out of my mind. So I gave in and made it."

"How is it?"

"I have no idea." For a moment, he appeared uncertain. "I was hoping you would tell me."

Her heart melted. "Okay."

"Okay, you'll eat my cobbler?" Colt's brown eyes sparkled.

"Wow, that sounds slightly dirty," Tracy teased. "Yes. I can't wait to eat...your cobbler."

He straight-up laughed as he handed her a fork.

"Right out of the pan?"

"No plates. Improvise when necessary." Colt shrugged.

Tracy gingerly dipped the fork into the edge of the crust. She didn't eat a lot of baked goods. Gluten-free was more accessible these days but she'd just gotten out of the habit. The crust crumbled slightly, flaky and buttery. She scooped a bite into her mouth.

The flavors burst on her tongue: tart, sweet, earthy. The crust had a slightly nutty flavor. "What is that nutty taste?"

"It's the buckwheat." He held the skillet in both hands like an offering to the gods, his body vibrating with pent-up energy as he waited for her judgement.

"It's...amazing." She licked her lips and dug the fork in again. Oh goodness. It had been way too long since she'd had apple cobbler. She'd forgotten how much she liked it.

"What's the verdict?"

"I love it."

The tension in his body eased at her compliment. "For the past year, I felt like a limb had been amputated. Off balance and unco-ordinated. But today it was like it was re-growing while I worked in the kitchen."

"That's wonderful!" She squeezed his biceps, her brain flipping back to when he'd carried her from the laundry room to her cabin.

Her cabin that was unusable and about to be under construction.

The only good news was that the apparent water leak, the reason she needed to leave, hadn't invaded her cabin yet. Her laptop and printer were undamaged. Thank goodness. Because there was no way she could afford a new one right now.

He had a look of anticipation on his face. As if the commentary on his food was not the only answer he was waiting for.

She'd already told him about his food. He had also offered her a place to stay. "You're sure?" She really couldn't afford to stay at a more expensive place.

Once again she wondered how people did it. How did they survive when catastrophe struck?

People were friendly here. No question they were more friendly than people in the city. But staying with him still seemed like an awful big imposition.

"It's only for a day or two, right?" Colt waved away her unspoken concerns. "It's no big deal."

"Yes. Only for a day or two."

And that was how the political heiress turned gastropub waitress in hiding ended up living with a cranky, famous chef.

(12)

COLT

Cee-Cee followed him home with her rental car.

"You know you could save some money by turning in the car," Colt suggested as he lugged her Louis Vuitton suitcase toward the cabin. He couldn't miss the fact that money was an issue.

"I'm not paying for the car. My friends rented it for me."

If she had friends willing to shell out money for a rental car, why wasn't she staying with them? But he kept the question to himself.

She answered as if he had spoken. "I...needed to get away for a few days."

Except she'd been in Colebury for over a week. And she didn't seem like she was in any hurry to leave.

They entered the small sitting area of the cabin. The compact design and layout created little mini separate areas making the place seem bigger than it was. She soon made herself at home, with a sheaf of papers on the coffee table and her bag near the day bed, unzipped with clothing spilling out the sides. She dropped a giant leather makeup bag on the tiny vanity in the small bathroom, reminiscent of his sister's plethora of cosmetics.

Colt looked around the cabin with bemusement. She'd been here less than an hour and bits of her presence were everywhere.

Even the queen-sized day bed with the wrought-iron frame hadn't escaped the whirlwind that was Cee-Cee. She'd dropped a floppy white beach hat over one finial.

Her spending habits seemed to be all over the place. That bag probably cost over a thousand dollars, but she was staying at the cheapest place around. Sometimes she seemed to forget that she needed to watch her pennies.

It was as if she didn't think about money until she had to pay for something. And then she carefully counted it out. That was unusual. Her clothes were high-end. Her attitude was high-maintenance. But there was an unexpected sweetness to her that was so genuine.

"Are you hungry?"

He waited for her answer, mentally reviewing what was in his refrigerator and thinking and discarding ideas for dinner.

"I could eat." Her stomach growled. "Or we could just gorge on dessert," she teased.

"We need sustenance."

He wanted to cook for her. Wanted to treat her. To make her the most amazing food she'd ever had.

With the exception of a few slices of wheat bread and some turkey, he had no food in the house. Then he realized it was Thursday. "Want to go to the farmer's market?"

"Uh, sure."

"I want to get some ideas for Chuck and Lottie's anniversary party. I like the idea of using locally sourced ingredients. They have spent their whole adult life here. We want to honor them and where they live."

A smile spread over her face. "That's wonderful."

They drove to the farmer's market in Colebury in his truck.

Being around her was...fun. He hadn't realized how much of his life lately wasn't fun. Ever since his meltdown, things had been somewhat grim. But within a few days she had managed to lighten up everything.

They drove to the town square and parked along the boulevard, walking through a park to get to a row of tents.

He hadn't felt this kind of creative urge in…years. Toward the end of his career, he'd been so focused on winning awards that his joy of cooking had gotten lost in a sea of competition. He focused on creating dishes that were over the top using exotic ingredients relying on unusual foods rather than solid cooking.

But suddenly ideas were flitting through his brain at warp speed. Just seeing the spread of produce and other food laid out before them, his brain was whirring. Flavor combinations popped into his mind and he wanted to grab up everything and rush back to his cabin to start cooking.

Instead, Colt forced himself to slow down and take in all the different foods available. They wandered through the market, winding through the tables and tents.

Colt had a method for discovery. First go through the rows and check out all the vendors and their wares. Then do a targeted run through the second time, stopping at all the booths and vendors whose products he wanted to buy.

He chatted with each vendor, asking questions about their methods and their products, storing away the information for later.

There were beekeepers. The Lyon Honey table, draped with the banner displaying their logo of a lion's head on a bee's body, was manned by a cute older couple who offered samples and recommended different specialties.

A cheesemaker's table was laden with pyramids of goat cheese, an extra sharp cheddar, and a soft brie. A forager had a table with various mushroom samplings. Colt grabbed some shitakes and chanterelles.

"I'll have to ask if Chuck eats mushrooms. I have a recipe for green beans, Dijon mustard, shitake mushrooms and black pepper, but I could adjust it."

There were several meat vendors and he contemplated picking up some pasture-raised chicken breasts and thighs for tonight's dinner or maybe he would do pork loin with a spice rub and an apple and dried apricot compote.

He bypassed the special spice rub offerings because he preferred to blend his own, but he made note of the meat vendors who ground their own sausages.

They skipped the tent with the freshly baked bread and another with jugs of Shipley cider. He checked to see if Audrey or her husband, Griff, were here but the booth was staffed by some younger guys.

As they wandered, he picked up some honey, goat cheese, spinach, carefully selecting products as he went. His fridge was small so he didn't have a lot of space.

The band set up in the corner was belting out tunes from the sixties.

He grabbed Cee-Cee's hand and threaded their fingers together. They stepped in unison.

She glanced at him with a sweet smile. He was beginning to recognize her different moods. Sometimes her smile was all about projecting happy without the emotion behind it. Sometimes it was about projecting laughter and a shared amusement. Sometimes it was about a bland default face that didn't have any umph behind it.

But this one was his favorite. This smile said she was happy. She'd forgotten about image, about being perfect. She was just happy. But he had no idea why. "What are you smiling about?"

"It's good to see you so excited." Cee-Cee's face lit up with incandescence. "I can't wait to taste your creations."

"I can't wait to cook for you." The past year had been about healing but now he thought maybe he was ready for this next phase. Because he hadn't been this interested in living for a while. Suddenly life was a banquet again, and after a year of starving, he was ravenous.

TRACY

Tracy's heart was full.

The trip to the farmer's market was a revelation. Watching Colt's tactile response to the various foods was like a master class in food appreciation. He sampled the wares with a methodical precision using all his senses.

He studied it with his eyes. Then smelled, inhaling deeply and taking in the aromas before tasting the food. Then he chewed slowly trying to soak up all the flavors and tastes in each item.

What struck her the most was his absolute absorption in the task.

After they went back to his cabin, she sat in the "living room" area with her laptop while he created his masterpieces.

The entire one-room cabin consisted of a living room area with a queen-size iron day bed, coffee table, a television stand that held a small twenty-inch Roku TV. The kitchen was literally one long counter with a sink, a tiny European range with two burners and a narrow oven, and a single drawer dishwasher. The fridge was an old-fashioned Smeg in a mint color. The countertop was a pale gray Formica.

She was embarrassed to admit that the entire kitchen would fit in her pantry. And she didn't cook.

Tracy sat on an upholstered wing chair next to Colt's day bed and watched as he moved around the kitchen in a choreographed dance, his hands sure and steady as he chopped and diced. A sauce simmered on the stove, scenting the entire cabin with spices. They'd picked up a small set of cookware at the hardware store on the way home.

It had felt momentous. As if he were taking a huge step into the present. But she knew better than to make a big deal about it. She didn't want to upset his delicate balance. Wasn't that why she kept trying to leave him alone?

Colt was in his element, his face a study in concentration as he tasted a savory and sweet sauce and browned the pork loin in a large cast iron pan.

"You want help?" she asked reluctantly. She had no idea what she could do to contribute but she would help if he asked. Maybe she could hand him things.

"Nope. I've got this." He had a dish towel thrown over one shoulder and smudge of something on his face.

Goodness. Every woman's fantasy. A man who cooks. And he didn't just adequately cook. His food was amazing.

They settled into a quiet rhythm.

She wasn't sure that she'd ever had this kind of simple ease with someone she'd just met. Normally she felt compelled to keep the conversational ball rolling but Colt was lost in his preparations and she needed to go through her emails.

Tracy plowed through her correspondence, deleting any that came from reporters. Yolanda had sent her the report from the private investigator. She read through the investigator's report on Esme.

He had had to dig deep. The background check that Fairy Tale Beginnings had run on Esme had come back without any red flags. But using his PI magic he'd discovered that Esme had done a ton of research on her brother. Apparently her online history was full of articles about both Thomas and the Thayer family. She'd paid someone to clean up her credit report and to smooth over some other incidents in her past. Tracy wasn't even sure what Esme's end game was. Except maybe to extort money.

The private investigator was still digging but the first round of information had been eye opening. She'd clearly gone to a lot of trouble to camouflage her real background.

That reminded her to text her brother:

Tracy: *How are you?*

Thomas: *Still reeling from the betrayal of both my fiancée and my sister.*

Tracy's heart clenched.

Tracy: *I didn't betray you.*

Thomas: *You omitted a critical piece of your life. Now I understand why you were always so busy. I can't believe you didn't tell me about this app.*

She picked up her cell phone. "You mind if I call my brother?"

"Go ahead."

She dialed her phone. "I'm sorry." She said before he could say hello.

He sighed. "I know."

They'd grown up more like twins, their births less than a year apart. Technically he was older, nine months barely, but they operated more like equals than older sibling/younger sibling.

After growing up together, as adults their lives took different paths.

Thomas had embraced the political arena. He'd been groomed his entire life to continue in the family business. Tracy had been working part time for her father since she was out of college, but she tried to stay out of the spotlight. She enjoyed the marketing and social media and the event planning. The spinning and the constant need to consider how actions could be perceived and whether it would poll well with voters she hated.

Being Cee-Cee had been freeing. She'd been able to relax and think about what she wanted to do. Not what was politically expedient.

"You doing okay?" she asked.

"I'll get there."

She wondered what had gone wrong with Esme. "Did she say why she left?"

"She was expecting some glamorous life of parties and yachts and other sh—stuff."

"So my suggestion to have quiet dinners in was not good?"

Thomas had been really busy on the campaign trail. He'd taken a leave of absence from his law firm to focus on campaigning and the upcoming election. Strong relationships were forged in the quiet times and in the stressful times. Tracy had assumed that Esme would prefer to spend time alone to cement their young relationship.

"Apparently she'd rather be jetting to Europe for the weekend."

"She clearly doesn't have a good grasp of what your life is really like." For one thing, obvious displays of wealth were considered both gauche and in bad form as a politician.

"No shit," Thomas said tiredly. "She brought up Muffy's birthday party."

Tracy shuddered. Her cousin Muffy had had a completely over-the-top sixteenth birthday party about ten years ago. The pictures had been splashed all over *People* magazine and other tabloid papers. They had spotlighted Thomas and Tracy in the articles because their dad was more famous than his brother, her uncle, Seth.

"We'll get through this." She decided not to bring up the fact that she had a private investigator looking into Esme's background. At this point, Tracy wasn't sure it mattered. Their family couldn't afford for Esme to reveal their closely held secret. Because if she did, no amount of spin could put that genie back in the bottle. As much as Tracy wished the truth could come out, the secret was not hers to tell.

The private investigator was digging further but there was nothing that Tracy could do until they had more information. Of course, they were also looking into Esme and Thomas's app counselor. Tracy prided herself on the personal touch. The client liaisons had training and knew there were steep penalties for divulging client information. Whenever people were involved, the human factor meant there was a window for corruption and bribery but the company screened carefully and they paid well.

"I'm tired of being alone, Trace."

"I know," she said softly. Sometimes she missed the days when it was the two of them against the world. "I'm trying to figure out what went wrong."

Because she believed that somehow her app had been gamed.

"It doesn't matter. We're in damage control mode right now." Thomas sounded defeated. "We're going to pay her off so she doesn't reveal you know what."

"I can't believe you told her."

"At some point we've got to find a way to trust. I just made a bad choice," Thomas grumbled. "I knew I shouldn't have used that matchmaking service."

"It's worked for plenty of people."

"But we aren't plenty of people."

That was true.

"Love you, T."

"You too."

She hung up with her brother and stared at the coffee table pensively, wondering what else she could do to help.

"Everything okay?"

"My brother's fiancée left him."

"Ah." Colt continued to stir the sauce on the stove. "Did you have anything to do with setting them up?"

What? How could he know? "Not exactly."

"Then it isn't your fault." Colt tried to make her feel better. "Sometimes people just aren't meant to be together."

But she felt guilty because she'd been pinning her own hopes on Thomas's marriage.

Her family had done a lot of good over the years. The Thayer Family Foundation, founded by her great-grandmother, focused on helping families and funding early education programs.

Her grandmother continued the administration until she

retired, and then Tracy's mother became the driving philanthropic force behind the foundation.

Tracy had no desire to continue on that path. She'd been hoping that Esme would take on the next generation of Thayer involvement so that Tracy could opt out of becoming the figurehead.

She'd felt trapped and locked in by generational expectations based on the circumstances of her birth. She was active in the organization, but she had no desire to run it.

However her experience in Colebury had opened her eyes to the precarious plight of working women and working parents. She really had no idea of how out of touch she'd been with the average person until she started living like one.

Colt had gone back to cooking, humming a Latin tune while he moved around the miniscule kitchen with ease, his movements so unlike the jerky uncoordinated efforts from the soup experience.

His hips swiveled and rocked as he sniffed and sauteed and tasted his creations.

Of course this wasn't exactly the average person's reality either. She was sitting in a small cabin in Vermont while a world-class chef prepared her dinner.

13

TRACY

They ate at the tiny drop-leaf table by the window. The evening sunlight blazed over the trees in the distance. The window was open and the gentle breeze ushered in the sounds of peace and silence. Someone must be having a bonfire because woodsmoke drifted in the air.

Colt had picked some more daisies and set them in an old glass bottle with a rubber stopper lid. The cheerful flowers and linen napkins and bright Fiestaware ceramics were all backdrop details. The food was the star of the evening.

"This is amazing."

"Happy to see you eating."

Tracy put down her fork. "What does that mean?"

"Just that sometimes women don't eat."

She watched her diet, for sure, and worked hard to maintain a healthy body weight. But she also acknowledged that genetics played a part. "I love food." Celiac had made her far more conscious of her food choices than plenty of people.

"I used to get really frustrated with customers who wanted to change the dish." The confession burst out of him. "The flavors are all wrong if you omit an ingredient. And I took that personally."

"Some people can't tell the difference. And some people," she gestured to herself, "literally can't eat it the way you imagined, without getting sick."

"Somehow I lost the pleasure of nourishing people and connections. Caught up in my own hubris." He stared out the window. "The act of eating together has become passé. My family ate together every night we could. Simple dishes but it was the together that mattered."

"Oh, that's nice. It was frequently just my brother and I."

"The one you were on the phone with?"

"The only one."

"Your parents worked a lot too?"

"They were gone off and on." She and Thomas had nannies and other staff who'd looked out for them. But for a long time it had just been her and her brother. No boarding school. They'd gone to a prep school but they'd gone home at night. Her father had avoided the appearance of having a lot of money. He'd actively avoided elitism and made it his life mission to look out for regular folks. They lived in a mansion but besides the giant house and the staff to maintain it, they lived what she had always assumed was a relatively modest lifestyle. Her parents drove mid-range American cars. They didn't throw lavish parties, unless they were entertaining political guests or foreign dignitaries.

"I used to be a pretty boring eater." They'd had to eat a variety of different cuisines when they'd been at dinners with visiting guests from other countries. So when it had been just her and Thomas, they'd had the staples.

"What was your favorite?"

"Macaroni and cheese."

"Something else you can't eat now."

She looked blankly at him.

"In addition to cinnamon rolls."

She'd forgotten.

"In the grand scheme of things, having to avoid certain foods isn't a great tragedy." She'd never had to worry about having food on the table. She'd been pretty damn lucky.

"True." He smiled at her.

And she smiled back.

"My turn to clean up." Then Tracy looked at the miniscule kitchen. There were pans everywhere, piled on the stove and the counter. She blanched.

He laughed at the look on her face. "I'll help."

Colt ran a sink full of hot soapy water. They washed the dishes together.

Dinner had been amazing. And the conversation had been fun. Being Cee-Cee had freed her from her normal constraints. She hadn't worried about what she could or couldn't say. She hadn't considered each word before she spoke.

She'd been honest.

Was that what Thomas had felt like while talking to Esme?

The relief at being able to tell the truth had been amazing. And she didn't want to stop.

"I hate lobster," she announced boldly.

"Okay. I promise never to cook lobster for you."

"Don't tell anyone." Then she had an instant hit of remorse. But the amount of relief that flowed through her was disproportionate to the magnitude of the admission.

Her father supported the fishing industry. It was vital to the state of Massachusetts and she understood that, but she had no desire to eat it.

"Your secret is safe with me." He laughed.

Oh my God it felt good to get that off her chest.

He raised one eyebrow. He probably thought she was a nut.

"Any other deep dark secrets you have a burning need to share?" He was teasing but suddenly she couldn't hold it inside any longer.

"When I was thirteen at a...dinner with my family I found out my mom was having an affair."

"Oh, shit." He squeezed her hand and threaded their fingers together. She held on tight. Tighter than necessary. But now that it had come out, she couldn't seem to stop.

"I saw them kissing. I was shocked. I adored my father. He was this larger-than-life figure and I couldn't believe that she could hurt him that way."

He didn't offer platitudes. Didn't try to explain it away.

She pulled her hand free and scrubbed at the dirty pan with fierce concentration. "It was like in a single instant my entire life shifted on its axis. I was adrift and confused. Everything I'd believed was a lie."

"What happened then?" As if he already knew her, knew that there was no way she could let that transgression lie.

"If I am the princess—"

"Ah so you come by that title honestly."

She poked him in the side, and he laughed. "—she was the queen." Tracy leaned against the counter, her hands sinking into the hot water as she stared out the little window over the sink. "I was devasted."

Her mother's actions weren't just a betrayal of Tracy's father but of their entire family.

She'd had a strong moral compass, a sense of right and wrong instilled in her from *both* her parents.

She remembered the conversation with her mother vividly.

"I'm going to tell Daddy."

"We'll discuss this at home. Right now you need to put on your public face and be a charming teenager." Her mother turned the knife. "You don't want to disappoint your father."

Tracy was a daddy's girl.

So the next day she'd gone to her father to talk to him. And her world was completely shattered when her father revealed that the marriage was a sham.

After she approached her father, he sat her down and laid out the facts of life. "Your mother and I have a relationship that works for us. It works for this family."

She decided then that she didn't want that kind of relationship. She'd stuck to that decision, but she also had never dated anyone seriously.

"Why do they stay together then?" His question jolted her out of her painful memories.

"Expectations. And weirdly their relationship works in every other way."

A fact she couldn't reconcile at thirteen, but now that she was an adult, she saw that they loved and supported each other. They just weren't in love with each other anymore. But she hated the lie that they perpetuated and that kept her trapped in a situation where she couldn't be honest with her own romantic partners.

"I guess this is where I whip out the NDA."

He snorted.

He thought she was kidding. If he only knew. But she would leave Colebury and he would never know who she was. He didn't read gossip magazines. And he didn't seem to be one to watch news. She'd caught him watching hockey at the Speakeasy but that was about it.

If she gave him a nondisclosure agreement he'd think she was nuts. Besides an NDA wasn't foolproof. After all, Thomas had Esme sign one. And if Esme revealed their family secret, even if they enforced the NDA it wouldn't matter. The secret would be out and the truth couldn't be denied. Years of silence and secrecy would be gone in an instant.

Most men would be uncomfortable discussing marriage issues after such a short time together. Maybe because it was temporary. Maybe because they both knew she would be leaving but there was no expectation or uncomfortable emotions associated with the fraught subject.

She shouldn't have even told him. But she'd never been honest with a lover in her life. And she didn't see how they were going to keep it a secret if Esme revealed what she knew about her parent's relationship.

So why shouldn't she take this moment and be completely honest?

Fortunately he moved on. "So that's why you're always trying to set people up?"

To balance out the scales. To help people find love and stay in love.

He wasn't being critical. He was just asking, but she felt defensive anyway. "I want people to find their fairy tale."

"Life isn't a fairy tale," he said almost immediately. "Love is messy and complicated."

"True. But there is such a thing as true love."

He smirked. "Now you sound like that ad for the dating app. Fairy Tale something."

That shut her up. She couldn't not be passionate about her company. And what did it matter if he dismissed true love? But she wanted to distract him.

"Have you ever used any dating app?" she challenged him.

"No time."

"That's exactly what they are for." She rinsed another pan with hot water. "So people can find partners that they are compatible with."

"Compatible?" He snickered. "Relationships need more than compatibility. They need heat and spice and smoking hot sex."

"Sex isn't everything," she pushed back.

He pushed her up against the counter, crowding her as the heat rose off the sink full of water.

His eyes were heavy-lidded as he trailed his scarred fingers over her collarbones. "You don't think heat is important?" His voice was husky as he pressed kisses along the side of her neck.

"Sure…it is," she said breathlessly, her body responding to the sensual subtext in his words.

"Sex is like cooking. The right ingredients and the right amount of heat and blending the two transforms them into something new and wonderful and unique."

Her body lit up like the fireflies buzzing around the orchard.

She wrapped her fingers in the belt loops of his cargo shorts and held on.

He held her captive against the counter.

"Then I guess I'm in trouble," she joked. "Since I suck at cooking."

He laughed. "You just need to practice."

The sounds of the crickets drifted in from the open window. The soft light of the setting sun coming through the curtains bathed the single room in a hazy, ethereal light, making the moment feel surreal.

Her heart sped up as he continued to drop slow kisses over her body.

COLT

Colt couldn't remember the last time he'd had so much fun.

His nose was a bit sunburned from the bright summer day, his kitchen smelled like heaven, and his arms were full of the most intriguing woman he'd had the pleasure to spend time with in...ever.

She was laughing, her blue eyes bright with amusement.

He wanted to submerse in that dazzling sunshine feeling and let it brighten the dark corners of his soul.

She was the catalyst who had brought him back to life.

His mood shifted, and he needed to consume her with an urgency that took him by surprise. "I need you." His voice was gravelly, his hands cupped her face, and he stared into her suddenly somber gaze.

She nodded. "Me too."

"Now," he demanded, overcome with an unexpected urgency.

"Okay," she said breathlessly.

He lifted her in his arms and carried her the few steps to the wrought-iron day bed. He shoved aside the worn patchwork wedding ring quilt and lay her on the soft blue sheets.

He followed her down and slipped the straps of her top off her shoulders. Her face was flushed from today's sun.

"You are so beautiful, *querida*."

She shrugged and looked away. "Genetics."

"You have a *grande coração*."

"What does that mean?"

"You have a big heart." He turned her face so he could look at her. "Inside. Where it counts. Your soul is pure."

At that she flushed. "I'm just me."

"*Graças a deus*." He kissed her, tasting the spice from dinner and the sweet of her flavors.

She arched up into his touch, scraping her nails along his back and then grabbing his ass. His erection prodded her.

"You taste of sunshine and strawberries." He kissed her again. "Hmm, the most erotic of flavors. You are all woman."

His lazy exploration erupted. Suddenly he was ravenous, starving for her.

She rubbed against his erection. His heart was pumping with a desperate need to be inside her. But everything about their previous sexual joinings had been frantic as if they didn't grab onto each other right away, the moment would disappear.

He slowed, kissing his way down her body. Tasting her skin, discovering the dips and valleys.

He brushed a wisp of hair from her cheek. Curling his fingers around her ear and cupping her head to press a soft kiss to her mouth.

Her cheeks were flushed. Her lips red and swollen from their kisses. Shadows lengthened, creating an intimate mood in the little cabin.

A swell of affection rolled through him. "What a perfect day." The trip to the market, the sunshine, and the sumptuous dinner, and now he had a warm, willing woman in his bed.

"I can think of a few ways it could be even more perfect," she snarked.

He chuckled against the swell of her breast. He cupped her in his hand and savored her. "I'm open to suggestions."

"Let's play...farmer's market."

He pushed up from his lazy exploration of her body. Studied the smirk on her face. "Okay. You'll have to teach me the rules."

She pushed against his shoulders, and he complied with her unspoken request to roll onto his back.

She stripped off her clothes so she was naked above him.

His shorts were still wrapped around his knees, holding him captive. But to get them off he'd have to move her and he wanted to see what she was going to do next.

"First, you meander down the rows." She kissed her way down his neck, trailed her tongue across his collarbones, skimmed her hands over his biceps with a light touch.

"Sample the merchandise." She sucked on one of his nipples then moved to the other.

He hummed as she used her tongue.

"Ask pertinent questions."

"Ah, like what?"

She continued down his body, spending a moment to swirl her tongue in his belly button. "Do you like this?" She kissed the hollow between his hipbones.

He groaned. "Yes."

"Or this?" She sucked the head of his cock into her mouth, her tongue doing things that might be illegal. She released him with a pop. "I need data so I can make an informed decision."

"I like whatever you want to do." She'd get no pressure from him.

"I'm asking for comparison." She curled her hand around him and pumped. He got even harder, the rush of blood almost painful.

"Okay, yes, go down on me," he ground out.

"With pleasure." And she swallowed him whole, working him hard with her mouth and hands.

She straddled his legs, her head bent, her blond hair mussed and swinging in her face. Her lips were slick as she took him inside.

The picture was a goddamn treasure. She was a treasure.

"Are you wet for me?" he ground out, trying to hold back his orgasm.

She moaned and nodded as she bobbed. Her eyes drifted closed with a blissful look on her face as if she were enjoying a decadent dessert. And he knew he needed to be inside her.

He jackknifed up and lifted her over his body. "I want inside you."

Her hands clutched his shoulders, and her breasts, pink and flushed, hung in his face. "Can't wait."

He blindly reached for the drawer in the small end table and prayed for condoms. They'd used up the packages from the motel laundry room. He clutched a package in his fist in triumph. "Yes!"

"Crow later. Get that on." Her words were breathless as she shoved his shorts to his ankles and pushed them off with her toes.

"Impressive moves."

"God, get inside me," she demanded.

The imperious tone turned him on even more.

"Happy to oblige." He rolled the condom on and slid inside in one smooth easy glide.

The urgent need to penetrate and dominate eased. He still wanted to mark her as his, the feeling primitive and raw. But once he got insider her, he felt as if he had come home and everything was right with his world.

Which sounded way too fanciful and weird.

Then she murmured, "Like coming home."

She felt it too. This inexplicable connection that had him sharing and doing things that he couldn't even have imagined a few weeks ago.

Colt began to move, his cock swelling as she surrounded him with her scent and her essence.

They went together like Beaujolais and Coq au Vin, a classic culinary pairing that had been around for centuries.

She rocked on top of him, increasing the pace, her body slick with arousal she took him in. The leisurely pace obliterated by the tide of desire threatening to swamp him.

They banged together frantically, no finesse or tender moves now. As if they couldn't get enough.

She squeezed her channel around him and the move sent him over the edge. He pumped into her in hot, urgent strokes, his orgasm a tsunami, making him dizzy.

His orgasm triggered hers and she threw her head back. Her nails dug into his shoulders as she rocked into him.

She dropped on top of him as if she'd wrung out every drop of energy and couldn't even hold up her head. Their hearts thundered in unison. Sweat slicked their skin. He kissed the side of her head and wrapped his arms around her, wondering how he could be so full of joy and so very spent at the same time.

14

TRACY

Tracy woke slowly the next morning in a strange place.

The soft pink light of early morning filtered through the lace curtains facing the orchard. She rolled and burrowed her head under the pillow.

Cobwebs and lack of sleep made her fuzzy because they'd had sex all night long. She smiled sleepily as the night played out in 4K resolution in her memory. She'd shared things with him that she'd never dared with anyone else.

But he'd shared things too. His fears about fame and his absolute reluctance to ever go back to any situation where he was in the public spotlight.

She understood his vehemence.

She understood everything about his intent to stay far away from the press and public scrutiny. And she realized that she couldn't bear to do anything that would hurt him.

She knew she needed to pull away...except she was staying in his cabin.

She was tired of hiding. She wanted to defend her choices. She didn't want to leave Colebury, but she didn't want to keep hiding either.

This whole thing was ridiculous.

But the break from reality had shown her that she was done with working for her father. She wasn't going to give away or shut down her business.

She wanted to focus on Fairy Tale Beginnings and the spin-off businesses.

Working in Colebury had given her ideas for how to move the company forward, how to make the app more accessible, and other services that they could be offering.

Even though there had been some backlash, clients from Fairy Tale Beginnings had fought back and posted online testimonials about how happy they were with their matches. Her marketing department had created an ingenious campaign using positive images and hashtags to combat the negative press.

All the fervent praise had convinced her that she was doing the right thing with her life.

"Good morning." His voice was soft, sleepy. "What's going through that brain of yours?"

His arm was wrapped around her waist, her hair was a tangled mess obscuring her vision, and she wanted to just savor this moment.

Last night had been magical.

Not for the sex, but for the intimacy.

But with everything he shared, she knew that she should pull away. She lay her arm over his and squeezed. "Last night was... really nice."

"Why does that sound like you're getting ready to say goodbye?"

Because she was. Her heart hurt.

Before she could voice what she was thinking, he said, "I reject that decision."

"It's for the best."

"Whose best?" He rolled her over so that she lay on top of him. "Not mine."

She pulled away but Colt pursued her. "I'm trying to save you from yourself."

But she had to be honest and admit that she loved his refusal to let her pull away. Even though she really was trying to save him.

She needed to go back to Boston soon. But maybe after her scandal was over, he would want to continue to see her. She loved that he had continued to pursue her, even against her own reservations and her attempts to save him. Maybe he would want a relationship with her when this was all over and she returned home.

Boston wasn't that far from Vermont.

Maybe they could make it work. Hope blossomed in her heart.

"Have you had a good time the past few days?" he asked.

She refused to lie. "Better than good."

"Me too," Colt admitted. "I like you. Your sunshine and your spirit make me feel whole again."

No one had ever said anything like that to her before. No one had ever really wanted *her*. She swallowed, overcome with emotion.

She wasn't sure it was her that had caused his shift. "You were working your way towards it." She just happened to be around when he'd begun to feel alive again. He'd shown her how to enjoy life. "You've shown me how to relax. So I think we're even."

Not that she was keeping score. But she should go. The problem was she didn't want to leave.

"What if I ply you with delicious food?"

Oh, she wanted to be plied by him. The offer was super tempting. And she was thrilled that he wanted to make her food. "It's wonderful that you're cooking again."

"You inspired me to get over that hump. You're my muse."

She loved the sound of that. She wanted to be his muse. She

wanted to burrow in this bed and not come out for the next month. But that was unrealistic. On several levels.

A seed of optimism took root in her soul. What if she could find a way to have Colt and everything else? Would he stay with her?

The amount of longing she felt for that possibility was immense.

She rolled over. "You really want me around?"

A lot of the people she hung around with enjoyed her connections. Having a political family meant that her family had influence. Her friends enjoyed her company, she worked hard at being likable, but they enjoyed the perks of her friendship more.

Her pals from the BBC were the exceptions, but they didn't hang out all the time.

And she was always on guard. She could never truly be herself, could never be completely honest. Maybe no one else felt the lack, but she knew it was there. Always holding back. Always watching her words.

She was the perky one. The happy one.

But with Colt she had the confidence to know that he wasn't using her for what she could do for him. He had no idea that her family was influential.

He liked her for *her*.

And he didn't care when Cee-Cee was snarky. She made him laugh.

However, "A muse sounds sort of intimidating."

Lots of expectations. Lots of things he would need her for that were all about him. People didn't put Tracy first. She came down the list.

It wasn't that she didn't have friends. And it wasn't that they didn't like her. She was eminently likeable. But people didn't put her first. Ever.

Colt snorted. "Only you would say that." He ran his hands over her arms and her waist, moving until he cupped her butt. His erection nudged her sex.

She was pretty sure they needed more condoms.

"Fine. I like having you around." He cupped her breasts in his large, scarred palms.

"I like being around," she confessed.

"So why not enjoy this while it lasts?"

God. She wanted it to last forever. But that was unlikely. "I may need some convincing."

He was silent, his head tilted to the side as if he were thinking deeply.

"What are you musing about right now?"

"A tasting menu."

Should she be disappointed that he was thinking about food? He'd started cooking again, supposedly thanks to her. So maybe she should just enjoy that fact instead of being disappointed that she was naked and he was thinking about food.

"It's just for me."

"That doesn't sound very hospitable."

He lifted her breasts and licked each nipple. "The first course is Cee-Cee raspberries. An incredible delicacy that I just discovered." Then he pressed her breasts together and sucked.

Realization dawned. He was talking about tasting her.

He rolled her again so she was beneath him and he kissed his way down the center of her stomach, lingering on the dip in her belly button. "This is a specialty just for me." He trailed his tongue over her skin. "A sensual treat."

She loved this playful side of him. She would never have imagined that the gruff, grumpy guy in at the table behind her on that first day could be this light and carefree.

He dipped his fingers into her, her wetness coating his digits. "A rare delicacy."

"That's just for you," she said huskily.

"Yep. All mine."

She wanted to be all his and so she let him feast.

COLT

Colt's heart thundered as his body recovered from another intense orgasm.

The sense of panic that had come over him when she'd talked about leaving had been extreme. In that moment he'd been willing to do anything to keep her here. He'd managed to distract her to stop her from leaving.

And what a distraction.

They were entwined together, lying on their sides. The warm morning breeze blew in air laden with lilacs and honeysuckle; the birds and the insects chirped and buzzed bringing their song through the open window. The cabin was still mostly dark surrounding them in an intimate cocoon. The atmosphere hushed except for the sounds of their breath.

He didn't want to bring up the fact that being here wasn't her long-term plan but he was also curious about her and her life in Boston. However, if he led with that he was pretty sure that she'd freeze up and talk about leaving again.

She was wrapped around him, her head resting on his arm. He stared at her taking in the sexed-up look. He loved disheveling her. She was normally so put together that when she wasn't, he knew it was because of him. Like he'd stamped her with his presence. That made him want to beat his chest and howl at the moon. *Mine*.

"I probably look a mess," she said breathlessly.

That need to always look flawless must have come from somewhere. "I think you're perfect. Why are you always so concerned with your appearance?"

She shrugged and glanced away. "It's a thing in my family. Doesn't your family have expectations for you?" She bit her lip as if sorry she'd asked.

He couldn't resist the impulse to kiss her. So he did. After a few glorious minutes he reluctantly pulled away.

For a moment his brain was addled. But she made a come on

motion with her hand. Right. His family.

"Honestly. They just want me to be happy." His parents and sisters and brothers had called frequently since he'd become a hermit up here in Vermont. But they always ended their conversation with "We love you, be happy."

"What about yours?"

"I've been working in the family business which is what they want. But there are expectations that can be...constraining."

He sensed that there was a whole lot left unsaid. "What did *you* want?"

She was silent. "I wanted to make a difference. Which we're doing. But I also wanted something just for me. Which I did. But it turned out to be...complicated."

He wondered what the family business was but he also knew that if he pushed too hard, she'd be gone.

They were complete opposites. His Brazilian family was wild and chaotic while her family sounded buttoned up and restrained.

"So how do you let off steam?" Colt couldn't stop touching her. He trailed his fingers over her shoulders and down her arms, marveling at how soft her skin was.

She shivered and he wrapped her up in his arms.

"Dinner out. Occasional ball game. Tennis."

"With friends?"

"Sometimes. But most of the time it's a work function." She hesitated. "Although I have a group of close friends. We met during college at a business symposium. We're an odd bunch all with different interests and goals but I love them. And somehow we fit. They've been my rock."

But that made him wonder why she was in Colebury where she knew no one. "So how come you aren't with them right now? Not that I'm complaining because I am infinitely happy that you are in my bed."

She giggled. "We're all busy so we don't see each other as often as we used to. And several have paired off in the past year."

He heard the affection and the love in her voice. "But you've got them in your corner. Just knowing is reassurance."

She nodded in agreement.

"What about you?"

Plenty of his friends had made themselves scarce after the fiasco that was caught on tape. He'd been so angry at a sous chef during a competition that he'd thrown a ladle. Unfortunately it had landed in pan with hot grease, splattering his sous chef and burning him badly. Plenty of people who were acquaintances wanted nothing to do with him. He couldn't blame them. He'd been out of control.

"Honestly, I'd let most of my friendships fall away. I was too caught up in trying to get ahead that I didn't put in the time to stay connected."

"I never saw the video." She squeezed him tight. "Was it as bad as the press made it out to be?"

"Worse."

Luckily the sous chef had forgiven him.

But Colt had never forgiven himself.

"What about drinking?"

"Drinking started as a stress relief but at the end I was drinking all the time. Put me in a kitchen and I had a glass by my side."

"You haven't done that now." She commented.

She was right. Since he'd begun cooking again he hadn't even thought about taking a drink.

"That's good, right?" She looked hesitant.

"That's phenomenal." But would it last?

15

TRACY

After a couple of days off, it felt weird to be back in the Speakeasy. Weird but good.

She had missed the camaraderie and the busy-ness of the restaurant.

Mrs. Beasley had called and Tracy's old room was ready again. But Mrs. Beasley had slipped in that there was still one reporter hanging around.

On the way to work she'd made several phone calls.

Thomas had let her know that they had settled with Esme.

Tracy had also spoken with Bernie and her CEO. She could go back to Boston. But she didn't want to. She was happy here. She didn't want to leave this little slice of paradise, this respite from the pressures of her life. She'd gotten so much work done. She loved Colebury. She loved the people. She even had begun to love working in the restaurant. Even if she was terrible at it. She loved spreading joy.

And she loved being with Colt. Loved the ease of them. She still worried about what would happen if he found out who she was. But she had no intention of letting that information get out. She would leave Colebury before anyone discovered her identity.

Every moment they spent together she longed for their growing relationship to be real. For them to be a couple.

She loved everything about her life right now. Especially Colt.

She was falling for him.

Against her better judgment. He made her a better person. He challenged her on so many levels. They'd spent hours planning the party for Chuck and Lottie. She'd worked on the financial plans for her offshoot business while Colt spent hours creating new dishes. He'd picked up more spices and tinkered in the kitchen for hours. They'd worked in companiable silence as if they'd been living together for years instead of a few days.

Even with everything else in her life in chaos, she was happy.

How could she leave now?

"Hey, Cee-Cee." Anne bounced up to her. "What do you think of this? I'm thinking about selling it on Etsy." She wore a puffy headband with a silk flower glued above the right ear.

"Is it your design?"

"Yes." She beamed with pride.

"It's hitting all the right notes for the current fashion climate." Tracy pulled out her phone. "Hold still."

She snapped a picture. Then Tracy got Anne's Etsy store info and clicked the icon so she could load this post on her Fake Instagram feed.

It had been a few days since she checked her account. She flushed. She'd been far too busy banging Colt's brains out. When she logged on she was shocked to discover she'd gained over thirty thousand followers. Uh, what the what?

She blinked. She had no idea why.

She didn't have time to analyze it right now. But she'd definitely have to figure out what she'd done to gain that many followers.

Ty and Matteo were tending bar. Anne was working the floor with Tracy.

"You're back," Ty commented. "Your regulars are at table 15."

Regulars?

Chuck and Lottie were there.

"Hey, you two. Nice to see you." She was a terrible waitress. But she was really good with people.

"Cee-Cee. Lovely to see you again."

"Can I get you some lunch?" She'd forgotten the menus again. "Oh, let me get menus."

"No need. We're here to meet with Colt." Lottie beamed.

Colt?

"He made up some samples for us to try." Lottie rested her head on Chuck's shoulder, her eyes sparkling. "Our gin rummy friends, Iris and Rose, are joining us to help out. They are excellent cooks."

"That's wonderful."

"He made us our very own tasting menu."

Tracy flushed, thinking about the last time Colt mentioned a tasting menu. "Let me bring you some iced tea."

"Diet coke, dear. And one of Griff's ciders for Chuck."

"Right." Jeez, she should be able to remember at least one of their drinks. "I'll get that pronto." She popped over to the bar and smiled at Matteo. He was a single dad who had moved from New York to bring up his daughter in a small town. She admired his intentionality in putting his daughter first.

"How's that little girl?"

"Doin' good."

Tracy put in the request for the drinks and waited patiently.

Colt sauntered in a few minutes later with a big smile on his face.

She could feel an answering expression as he shot her a conspiratorial grin.

He held a wire mesh basket lined with colorful napkins and he had a folder tucked under his arm. He shook hands with Lottie and Chuck and they all sat down again.

Tracy leaned over the bar and quietly ordered an iced tea for

Colt with a small teaspoon of sugar. He had a full pitcher in his fridge, and she'd watched him fix his drinks over the past few days.

"You know what the chef man drinks?" Matteo raised an eyebrow and efficiently doctored Colt's tea.

She flushed and shrugged. "I'm observant."

He laughed. Hard.

Tracy frowned at him. Okay, maybe he was right. Just to be silly she added a lemon to Colt's tea. Maybe he wouldn't even remember their exchange about the day they met.

But when she plopped the glass in front of him, he grinned. "Thanks for the lemon."

"My pleasure," she said.

A couple of older ladies, one with silver hair and lavender streaks and the other with long white hair, blew in the front door and headed for their table. Lottie introduced Iris and Rose to her and Colt.

Tracy was on duty so she couldn't sit and gab with them but she could swing by while she was working the floor to help with planning. "Have you thought about a theme?" Golden wedding anniversary obviously. "Beyond the gold."

Lottie and Chuck shook their heads.

"Celebrating fifty years in Vermont?" That wasn't quite right.

"I culled the best of ingredients from the farmer's market, but you'll have to let me know if there's some local delicacy that I missed." Colt continued explaining each item.

They tasted the treats, and Tracy stopped by periodically to hear them praising Colt and his cooking skills as they oohed and ahhed over his offerings. She filched a few bites and they were amazing.

That was a given. Because holy heck could the man cook.

But his simple pleasure in their compliments was a revelation.

"He's great, isn't he?" She couldn't resist commenting to the table.

Iris and Rose glanced between Tracy and Colt. "He certainly is."

Tracy thought she was missing something but she needed to get back to work. The Speakeasy was hopping.

After Chuck and Lottie and their friends left, Colt sat at a square table near the stage and lazily watched her hustle around. She knew what he was thinking by the heated look in his eyes.

And all was right with her world.

An unexpected peace blanketed her. She realized...she was happy.

Her hot boyfriend had rocked her world this morning and then shoved her happily out the door to head to work. She thought the media furor over her app was dying down.

After a call with her attorneys, she had spent the better part of the past few days working on the paperwork to set up the spin-off businesses into their own entities, finally able to lay claim to the ideas without hiding.

The experience had been freeing.

Anne walked by and fanned her face. "Holy moly, you two are hot."

Tracy blushed. "I don't know—"

"Yes, you do."

Tracy flitted around the dining room, getting orders wrong and still managing to keep a smile on her customer's faces. It was really busy today.

Anne commented. "We're getting a lot of out-of-towners. We've got customers coming from as far as Boston to try the cremini sliders and the Shipley cider fondue you posted on Instagram."

What? That was great for the Speakeasy.

Everyone here was wonderful. The owners were chill and the gastropub employed a bunch of people. It was a win. But she really didn't want interlopers from Boston coming to her retreat. She wasn't quite ready to come out of hiding yet. She knew she'd have to reconnect with her real life soon but for now she wanted to enjoy living here.

As if she'd conjured them, her friends D'Andre and Elise walked into the Speakeasy with their baby girl in tow. Oh shit. Tracy stepped to the side and tried to hide behind Anne and her headband.

But Anne foiled the attempt by heading toward the beverage station.

Colt gave Tracy a strange look. The heat from earlier replaced by a frown.

"Tracy?"

Could she pretend not to hear them and head for the kitchen? Maybe...but she wouldn't do that to her friends. The moment she'd been dreading had finally happened. She was recognized. And it was her friends by some weird coincidence.

In any other situation, Tracy would have been happy to see them. They didn't get out as much since the baby was born.

They made a beeline for her.

"Hey." Her smile was forced as she hoped that no one was paying attention to them. But D'Andre Smith was a six-foot-four former wide receiver who was completely jacked. Her giant Black friend looked like he could still play football and he rarely went unnoticed.

"Well, look what the cat dragged in. It sure is good to see your smiling face." D wrapped his free arm around her shoulders and squeezed. "We've been worried about you." He glanced around the Speakeasy and took in the surroundings.

"Let's get you seated." Preferably in a corner, far away from the action in the main part of the dining room, where they could sit away from prying eyes.

"Are you...working here?" The deep sound of D's voice trailed off as he took in Tracy's uniform. The inexpensive Levi's and the black T-shirt with the Speakeasy logo.

Tracy smiled sunnily. "Yes." She led them to a table out of the way, wondering the whole time how they ended up in the town where she was working. "What made you come to Vermont?" It was quite the coincidence that they ended up in her little town, in her gastropub. She'd known she couldn't hide away forever but she'd been happy and enjoying that quiet life and really had not expected to see anyone she knew.

Elise snickered. "Jay was going to take everyone out on the yacht. So D suggested we hightail it out of town."

Tracy laughed. D was notoriously seasick. For such a big rough tough guy, he usually spent half the boat time hanging over the side.

"Naw. Elise saw a post about this place on Instagram and we decided to take a little trip," D rumbled. "Some account she started following that she said had genius posts...."

"Cider donuts." Elise had a look of bliss on her face. "I read an article last week about apple orchards and all the yummy food in Vermont and got a craving for cider donuts."

But there were plenty of orchards closer to Boston than Colebury, Vermont.

D held their daughter Mary cradled in his right arm, far more gently than he'd held a football. He was staring at Tracy as realization dawned on his face. "That you?" D asked.

She knew immediately what he was talking about. Elise had seen her Finsta and they'd ended up here.

Tracy nodded. Oh goodness, what were the odds? Elise worked in PR so she followed a variety of social media accounts. They'd had discussions about social media and how to amplify posts. It wasn't completely out of the realm of possibility, but it was still kind of a coincidence.

"I have friends who've used—" Elise dropped her voice low and leaned closer "—Fairy Tale Beginnings." She gushed, "They loved it."

Tracy was filled with pride.

"Guess I wasn't the only one hiding shit." D shook his head. "Girl, you've been keeping a lot of secrets."

Tracy flushed. "Just the one."

"Pretty damn big one." D raised one eyebrow.

She glanced around the restaurant, hoping no one heard what they were discussing.

Colt watched cautiously from his table in the corner. How could she fix this before it became a complete disaster?

Her stomach turned.

Because then disaster happened. Colt stood and sauntered over to their table. "D?"

Fabulous. He knew D'Andre. Her life was about to get a whole lot more complicated.

"Hey, man." D and Colt did some complicated handshake thing. "How you doin'?"

Holy moly. They clearly knew each other *well*. Could this get worse?

"Pretty good."

"You look great." D studied Colt while Tracy just wanted to disappear into the kitchen and maybe not come out...ever.

"Thanks. I'm doing well." Colt's look was slightly accusatory, and he didn't seem happy. "You never mentioned you knew D."

"It never came up." Her temper simmered, even though she knew she was in the wrong. She'd been lying to him about her identity since they met.

"Wait. You know Tracy?"

"Apparently I don't." Colt's words were biting.

Tracy's heart sank. Because he didn't know Tracy. He knew Cee-Cee. And he was pissed at her.

"Nice to see you, D." Colt nodded shortly at everyone else. "I'll leave you guys to catch up."

"So you've been keeping more than one secret," D'Andre chastised. "Why didn't you come to us?"

"My boss suggested that I get out of town." She put air quotes around *suggested*.

Elise snorted.

While they were talking, the rumblings had started. "Is that D'Andre Smith?"

"Oh my God, it is!"

D sighed. "I'd hoped this far away from Boston we'd be safe. Sorry, babe." He handed off the baby to Elise.

She smiled sympathetically. "Go do your thing and I'll chat with Tracy."

He dug a sharpie out of the baby's diaper bag. "I'll be back."

"What are you really doing here?" Tracy thought there had to be more to the story than they'd shared.

"I really did have a craving." Elise cooed at Mary.

"Oh my God, you're pregnant again?" Tracy brushed her hand over Mary's hair. The baby was an adorable mix of D and Elise with dark golden skin and dark curly hair.

"Shh, we aren't telling anyone yet."

"You just told me." Tracy's heart burst. Elise and D were one of her success stories. Although they didn't actually know that she'd expected them to get on so well when she engineered their meeting.

"We've been worried about you," Elise said softly.

Tracy had another thought. "You didn't figure out where I was, did you?" Because if her friends figured it out, a reporter or the press could do the same.

"Pretty sure Pete and Britt have known the whole time."

What?

Tracy dropped into the chair next to Elise. She was on duty, but Elise had just dropped a bombshell and all her customers were in line to get an autograph from D. "They told you where to find me?"

Elise nodded. "The general area."

The whole time she thought she was here all alone, her friends were out there thinking about her.

"They're still getting hounded by the press and they didn't want to potentially lead anyone here."

That made her miserable. She hadn't meant to bring this kind of scrutiny down on her friends.

"So we offered to come check on you."

Another thought occurred to her. "But how did you know to come to the Speakeasy?"

"I really do follow @ceeceeinthecountry." Elise laughed. "We stopped here for lunch. Then Pete was going to ping you on your email for us so we could find you."

Her heart warmed. After weeks of feeling alone, her friends had been looking out for her.

Elise glanced around the packed restaurant. "Bet you can't wait to get out of Vermont."

"It's beautiful here," Tracy defended.

"It is. But it isn't Boston," Elise said softly.

Elise was right. It wasn't the city. Yet she didn't really miss it.

"So—" Elise leaned forward in her seat, while Mary banged on the table with her little fists "—who's the guy?"

Tracy glanced at Colt but he was studiously ignoring her. And her heart broke just a little. "Colton Vega."

Elise blinked as if trying to place him. A bunch of patrons circled around D'Andre clamoring for autographs.

"Celebrity chef. Vega's in the city was his signature restaurant but he had a couple of others before he left Boston." Until he had his epic meltdown.

Elise nodded. "I vaguely remember reading something about it. But that look was more than just a celebrity chef you happened to meet."

Tracy kept her gaze away from Colt. She couldn't talk about him right now. "I have to get back to work."

"Why are you working here? You could probably buy this whole town," Elise joked.

Tracy ducked her head. "It's a long story." She grabbed a few menus and handed them to Elise. "Everything on the menu is really good."

Elise pressed a hand to her flat stomach. "How about a decaf hot tea?"

"I'll get it right away."

The crowd around D had started to dissipate. But the

customers had turned their attention to Tracy and Elise, wondering who he had come in with and who he had spoken with in the restaurant.

More rumblings started. Did someone recognize her?

"You should try the grilled cheese with the duck confit. It's to die for." She scurried toward the kitchen.

Other people in the restaurant were looking at Tracy as if they should know her. Crap. This was escalating quickly.

Then her worst nightmare came true. "Is that Tracy Thayer?" The damage had been done and there was nowhere to hide.

"Congressman Thayer's daughter?"

"Isn't she the one with the dating app?"

Conversations swirled around the dining room.

Anne and Matteo both stopped what they were doing to stare at Tracy. Matteo had paused mid swiping of the counter. Anne's mouth was hanging open. They'd been slightly awed by D'Andre but now they were looking at her like she was an alien.

The worst was Colt.

He seemed to instinctively realize she'd been discovered.

He didn't look happy about it when he realized she hadn't just lied about her name, and she wasn't just holing up to lick her own wounds, but that she'd been actively hiding from the public.

"Fairy Tale Beginnings is yours?" Anne said so loudly that the customers at the Gin Mill could probably hear her.

"You are that congressman's daughter? Aren't you like a billionaire?" Matteo pulled the tap and began filling the Pilsner glasses. "What are you doing working at the Speakeasy?"

She could feel Colt behind her.

She turned around slowly. Hadn't she just been thinking life was perfect?

He stood there with his arms crossed over his chest.

She ignored everyone else and just spoke to Colt. He was the only person here who mattered. "I...should have told you."

"The Thayers?" Colt flexed his forearms with a forbidding

frown on his face. "According to your family story, your parents have the ultimate fairy-tale romance."

He raised his eyebrows, silently asking *what the hell?*

Shit.

"That's my family," she said tightly. She had told him the truth. She could see the realization dawning in his eyes. He knew their secrets.

"You're the one they were looking for during that news piece a few weeks ago."

She nodded miserably.

She hadn't anticipated how terrible she would feel. He had the power to severely harm her family's reputation. But even more than that, he had the power to hurt *her*.

"Were you going to tell me?"

Before she could answer, a guy from one of the tables pushed next to her. "Tracy Thayer, I'd love to ask you some questions."

"You'll have to check with our media office if you want an interview." Her response was rote, involuntary and immediate. She didn't even need to think.

"They've been stonewalling for weeks and you are right here."

She and Bernie had hammered out what to say over the phone this morning. Thayers didn't speak with the press unless a carefully crafted statement had been preapproved.

But she didn't want to speak to the press right now. She wanted to clear things up with Colt.

She noticed how quickly Colt recoiled when he realized the guy was a reporter.

"No comment."

Colt snorted. "Good luck with that."

Everyone in the bar was listening. The murmur had died to a hush as she turned the reporter down.

"Come on. You're right here. Just one question." The reporter got in her face, shoving closer. "What did your father say when he found out you were running a dating service?"

"She said to leave her alone." Colt stepped between the two of them.

"It's okay." She put her hand on his forearm. "I've got this."

"Hey! I recognize you," the reporter said to Colt.

Colt's face closed up. He was mad. But he'd still stepped in to protect her.

In that moment Tracy's dream withered and died on the vine like a flower without water. She pulled the reporter's attention back to her.

"You want a statement?" She moved away from Colt so that the reporter would follow. But he continued to look back over his shoulder at Colt.

She didn't want to talk to a reporter, but in this moment, her only thought was to protect Colt.

"Follow me."

She led him away from Colt. And she walked away from the future she'd been dreaming of.

16

TRACY

The reporter turned around to look at Colt one more time.

"You get two questions." Tracy diverted his attention and led him up the stairs to the event space where Chuck and Lottie would have their anniversary party. She'd been hoping to stay until that happened, but now that it was out that she was here, her presence would be trouble she didn't want to bring to Colebury.

"You want to know my father's thoughts about the dating app? My father continues to be proud of the accomplishments of both me and my brother." Which didn't answer the spirit of his question, but that was his problem not hers.

"What do you say to the charges of elitism leveled by your father's opponent?"

This was not in the approved statement that Bernie had sent along but she was going to answer honestly. "I'd say, while that was not my intention, that he was correct."

The reporter blinked, clearly surprised at her answer. Especially after the previous non-answer.

"Fairy Tale Beginnings prides itself on doing intensive security background checks and discovery on our clients to make sure that they represent themselves properly. We also use a very sophisticated questionnaire system along with personal counselors. It is an expensive service to run and I priced the registration fee accordingly. But I acknowledge now that the fee prices out a significant portion of the population. We are going to take steps to address that."

She wasn't sure how. Her business model was based on the current pricing, but she also knew that things couldn't stand the way they were.

"What about Esme Taylor's accusations?"

"I won't comment on my family's private life. But I believe our family's commitment to championing the less fortunate and creating opportunities to help others speaks for itself. Actions are louder than any random person's words."

She'd love to out Esme for manipulating the system but that would only bring about more scrutiny. And that was the last thing they wanted.

That should be enough time for Colt to have disappeared.

She'd also love to tell the reporter to ask Esme but the condition of her settlement with Thomas was that she cease and desist from any more criticism or revelations about their family.

Tracy thought her parents should consider coming clean about their relationship. But that was their secret to tell.

"I gave you a bonus answer." She tried to pull out her marketing and press secretary persona and answer with a smile, leave them feeling good. But her mind was still back on the look of betrayal that Colt had leveled at her before he'd left. "And I've got to get back to work."

"You are actually working here?" His tone was so dismissive her hackles went up.

"They have the best grilled cheese and sliders around. And the cider is top-notch."

COLT

Colt was pissed.

He had to get out of here. He left the Speakeasy quietly. He wasn't about to make a scene. But his temper was simmering and the last thing he needed to do was be angry in public. And for a moment, he'd forgotten.

Cee-Cee was famous. No, not Cee-Cee. *Tracy*.

Tracy Thayer.

Everyone knew who the Thayers were. Her family was well-connected and prominent, like the Kennedys and the Bushes with generations of family in public office.

She wasn't just running from a crappy situation or taking a break from a stressful life. She'd been hiding out. From the press. From the public. She was famous—as in "in the tabloids and society pages and the *New York Times*" famous.

All the clues had been there, but he'd ignored them because she made him feel good.

Now she had brought the press down on him and the little town of Colebury. Her entire life was a fishbowl.

Things were coming back to him. Pictures of her cousin's sixteenth birthday party had been in *People* magazine. The party had not been that extravagant compared to some of the celebutants around at the time, but people were obsessed with her family.

His younger sister had kept that article about her cousin's sweet sixteen birthday party taped to her bedroom wall. He had probably looked at teenaged Tracy Thayer a million times before that picture came down.

His sister had gone through a phase where she wanted to be famous. She'd been the most thrilled when he'd been competing on cooking shows and hobnobbing with celebrities. She'd also been most contrite when it had all gone to shit.

Earlier when that reporter got in Tracy's face, he'd wanted to step in and vanquish the reporter for her. But he didn't even know what to say.

He couldn't go back to life in a fishbowl.

The thought of being a target for the press made him want to throw up. That initial hit of anger was a huge red flag. He was never going back to those feelings again. Not for anyone.

Not that she had asked.

He headed back to his cabin and waited. He assumed she'd come back there.

Although who knew. She didn't need the things she'd left at his place.

She was rich AF. He should get out and let her come by and pick up her stuff without him around. But he wanted to talk to her before she left.

Needed to hear why she'd continued to lie to him.

They had shared plenty of concerns and fears about life and she had never once mentioned that her family was famous. She had known that he would have been appalled.

He paced around the cabin, an abundance of restless energy pulsing through him.

He needed to do something to release the pressure cooker of his emotions.

Cook. He needed to cook. The meeting with Chuck and Lottie and their friends had been fun. He'd been inspired to try some new dishes.

A few hours later, after messing around in the kitchen—stress cooking, was that his new thing?—the dishes were plated and waiting for him to taste, but he didn't have an appetite. The food looked good, smelled great, and his stomach rolled at the thought of eating.

Colt heard her car come up the drive.

He sat on the day-bed, leaning back, hands clasped between his legs. He'd been sitting here waiting, so many things running through his mind.

He'd thought they'd been cultivating a bond but clearly she'd just been marking time.

She walked through the door and he drank in the sight of her. It would probably be the last time they spoke and he wanted to remember every little detail.

He wanted to stay mad at her, but the overwhelming emotion that crowded his throat and kept him quiet was sadness.

She'd brought him back to life.

Then she'd stabbed him in the heart.

"Hey," she said softly.

"What took you so long?" He'd expected her earlier.

"I finished out my shift."

"Why?" She didn't need the money. In addition to the generational wealth, she'd started an incredibly successful dating service.

"I couldn't leave Phoebe in a bind," she said tentatively. "And I spent a bit of time with D and Elise since they had come up to check on me."

Her famous wealthy friends.

"How do you know D?" she asked.

"We worked on a fundraiser for food insecurity in Boston a few years ago. Back when he was still playing football."

"Ah." She stood awkwardly just inside the doorway. "I'm sorry."

There were so many things to be sorry for. Did he actually care why she was sorry? He wasn't sure it mattered. But she seemed to be waiting for him to say something.

"I should have…." She began to wander aimlessly around the tiny cabin, not looking at him.

He wasn't in the mood to be forgiving. She hadn't straight-up lied, but… "There was plenty of time to mention your family was freaking political royalty."

She flinched. "True."

There was an unvoiced *but* her response.

"There was the scandal." About her dating app.

"And...." She nodded. "You're right. But once I told you, everything would have changed. And for just a little bit I wanted to be happy. To be Cee-Cee."

"Why give me, *everyone*, a fake name?"

"Because I was tired of being Tracy." She plopped down into the wing chair. "Cee-Cee is more relaxed, she tells people what she really thinks, she doesn't have to run her thoughts through a curated filter to make sure they don't offend anyone and piss off the wrong people."

"You're talking about Cee-Cee like she's real."

"She is real. She is me." Tracy's shoulders slumped. "The unfiltered version of me anyway."

So what was he? Just a dalliance while she was stuck in Vermont? He couldn't bring himself to ask.

She was leaving. Did it really matter?

"I was able to keep your name out of the statement." Tracy got up and started moving around the room, picking up her clothing and shoving items haphazardly into her Louis Vuitton bag. "The reporter recognized you after you left."

He shrugged. He was old news. Hopefully. Unless someone brought up his catering for the Speakeasy, he should be an oddity. A quick "where is he now?" and then he'd be forgotten again. Just the way he wanted it.

As long as he stayed out of the public eye, which would never happen with her around.

She zipped up her bag and then stood in front of him, twisting her hands together. "I need to ask you a favor."

He raised an eyebrow.

"I'd appreciate it if you would not tell anyone what I told you about my parents." She looked miserable. "In complete honesty, you could sell that information for a lot of money. But it would destroy my family."

Anger blazed through him. He had never been obsessed with money. Fame, yes. "You think money is what motivates me?" She didn't know him at all.

"No. I apologize for implying that." She shook her head. "But that is a closely guarded secret."

She was composed. Too composed. She had on her fake face. The one she showed to other people.

There was no smiling happening.

He shoved to standing and began to pace.

He wanted to let her off the hook but...she'd hurt him. And it really didn't matter to anyone, except him. "Why did you stick around so long?"

"My father's communication director wanted me out of sight."

He rejected that answer. She could have gone home at any time. "You always listen to him?"

"He was my boss."

"Was?"

"I'm quitting."

TRACY

Tracy was going to throw up.

Before she arrived back at the cabin, she'd held out a small hope that maybe they could work things out. That he would understand the rock and hard place that she'd been in and they could move forward together.

That his talk of her being good for him wasn't just talk. That he would stand with her.

But since she'd come inside the cabin he'd been distant and forbidding. She couldn't blame him. She understood and still her heart was crumbling.

"I guess I'll...go." She gestured to her bag in the corner. "I'll do one final pass and then get out of your hair."

She made a circuit around the small cabin. Surreptitiously she tucked his John Deere cap in her bag.

While she looked around for her stuff, she waited for him to ask her to stay. To say *don't go*. If he gave her any encouragement, she would fall to her knees in gratitude and promise to take the next fifty years to make it up to him.

"That would be best."

With those quiet words, her heart broke the rest of the way. She should have known that he wouldn't stick around.

That fantasy of him, of them, that she'd built up in her mind was just that. A fantasy. Fairy tales didn't exist. At least not for someone like her. Maybe she'd used up all her good karma with her ancestry. She was destined to be alone. Never trusting anyone enough to let them in. She'd trusted him and look where it got her. Her heart was broken.

"Question."

She whirled around, a small hope in her heart. "Yes?"

"Fairy Tale Beginnings is you."

She loved that he got that it was her. "Yes."

"All those times you connected other diners, the employees, whoever, was Tracy." Colt continued to analyze her actions dispassionately. "You didn't just connect people romantically. You put together those hikers."

"Sure. I love connecting people." It was what she'd done since she was a kid.

"So why haven't you ever tried to match yourself with anyone?" Colt studied her. "You couldn't find the right person?"

"I didn't use my app." Tracy shrugged. Told the absolute truth. "I could never be completely honest. That didn't seem right. How could I have a relationship when I was holding back an event that shaped everything about me?"

"Yet you didn't feel the need to be honest with me either."

Her heart dropped. She had been more honest with him than with anyone. But her secrets had the ability to hurt him. He'd told her how much he hated the spotlight, hated fame. And to protect herself she had withheld a crucial piece of information.

Sure, she'd tried to step back, but she hadn't tried that hard. Yearning for the connection that they'd had, thrilled when he'd pursued her. Because no one had ever wanted her just for her. There were always family considerations, family connections, in play when she met someone.

"I wanted to." But she'd feared exactly this. That he would turn away from her once he knew who she was, once he knew who her family was. She'd been more honest with Colt than with anyone else. Ever. Even her friends didn't know about her parents. But telling him that now would give him ammunition. Would give him more information to use against her if he chose.

"But did you?" He shook his head. "You're right."

"About what?"

"You can't have a relationship based on lies."

"If I could go back and have a do-over, I would."

"Yeah, well, you can't go back."

It was clear from the finality in his voice that he had no intention of going forward.

That's when she knew they were over.

17

TRACY

"You hooked up with Colton Vega?" Her pal Courtney roamed around the living room of her penthouse condo.

"Um, yes." *Hooked up* wasn't quite how she'd put it. *Immersed in, absorbed in, fallen in love with.* Those were all terms she would use to describe what happened with Colt. She had fallen in love with him. It only took a few weeks. Hopefully falling out of love would work on a similar timeline. But she wasn't counting on it.

"Man, I ate at Vega's a few years ago." Courtney twisted the rings on her fingers. "His food was the bomb."

Tracy stared out the window, watching a couple walking down the sidewalk of her residential neighborhood. They were wrapped up in each other.

Why couldn't she have that?

Her shoulders slumped.

Britt sat on the sofa, looking at her with concern. *You okay?* she mouthed.

Tracy nodded. She was miserable but she'd get over it.

Britt and Courtney had met Tracy at the rental car return place where she'd dropped off the small compact. The drive back to

Boston and her real life had only taken a few hours. She'd hopped on the highway and been back in the city, leaving Cee-Cee and Vermont behind her.

"Did he cook for you?" Courtney was a member of the BBC. She designed video games with kickass female lead characters. This week her black hair had bright pink streaks.

"Yes." And it had been amazing. Whatever else happened, she had helped him overcome his reluctance to get back in the kitchen.

"Court, maybe we should talk about something else," Britt said.

"Wow. Okay, you're sad. I'll quit talking about how amazing his food is." Courtney gave Tracy a hug. Beneath her tough-girl exterior, she was a total marshmallow. "He looked pretty good in that photo."

The reporter had snapped a picture of her and Colt before he'd approached her at the bar. He'd posted it without permission. Tracy had already had her lawyer send a takedown notice but who knew if or when it would actually be removed.

She'd left a message on Colt's cell phone and apologized. But he hadn't called back.

Hopefully after that one incident, the press would leave him alone.

She'd removed herself from his vicinity.

"He did." He'd been in profile. The moment that he'd discovered her secret had been immortalized in print. So that she could look at it and agonize all over again how much she'd hurt him. She was stupid but she'd saved the image to her computer.

She didn't have any pictures of him. Or them together. Except that one. Of course, that wasn't a bad thing. She didn't need to be mooning over his photo and wishing things could be different.

"Screw him if he doesn't appreciate you." Courtney made a slashing motion with her hand. But Tracy knew that was her frustration with her own man problems rather than any animosity toward Colt.

"He's a really good person." Tracy felt the need to defend him. "I lied to him. And he isn't interested in the notoriety and scrutiny my family would bring."

"You are not your family," Courtney shot back.

No. But the truth was more complicated than that. "He's a good person," she reiterated. Apparently, she just wasn't the right person for him.

"What can we do to make it better?" Britt asked.

She loved her friends. Solidarity. "Stop talking about it?" Tracy said desperately.

"Dude, we could talk about your business instead." Courtney plopped on the traditional French settee next to Tracy. "Now I understand why you kept trying to get me to try it out."

Courtney had her own guy problems. And Tracy didn't see them getting better any time soon.

"Tell us all about your brush with country life and living like the average person."

She knew Courtney was trying to tease her out of this funk, but that just made Tracy want to cry as well. "I had no idea how hard it would be for the average person to come up with the Fairy Tale registration fee."

Britt snorted. "I could have told you that ten grand was way out of reach for most people." She lived with Pete now but Britt had had her own money struggles last year.

"I can't talk about it yet." It hurt too much.

"I've got an idea." Britt pulled out a bottle of Dom Perignon. "Let's get drunk."

"Works for me," Courtney chimed in.

Britt popped the cork expertly and poured the golden bubbly liquid into several flutes.

Getting drunk wouldn't solve her problems, but maybe it would let her forget for just a few hours.

The next afternoon, Tracy headed to her parent's house in Welles-ley. Once she'd been discovered in Vermont and Colt had cut her loose, there had been no reason to stay.

Besides, now it was time to home and fight.

She could have returned sooner. Now she wished she had just left when she had been cleared to come home. She should have left on a high note.

She hadn't done anything wrong. Her app worked and matched couples. There was nothing nefarious or illegal about what she did. However, she'd gained valuable insight into the fact that Fairy Tale Beginnings wasn't accessible to a lot of people. She already started developing ideas to change that on her drive home.

The mansion had a separate wing that was strictly for her dad's work. Bernie also had an office in the wing. Tracy stopped in Bernie's office before going in search of her father. The wall-to-wall carpeting and ornate wood desk with Queen Anne chairs upholstered in a traditional Tudor pattern were all familiar to her. She'd grown up in this office. She looked around fondly, as she mentally said goodbye.

Bernie was there and they held a quick strategy session. Thomas had agreed to settle with Esme before she revealed the damaging information about her parents' marriage. Esme had put the registration fee on a credit card and bought clothing and spent money to transform into the ideal woman for Thomas. She wanted reimbursement for her expenses plus extra for the emotional distress of calling off the engagement.

Tracy had met with Pete and Yolanda this morning and figured out how Esme had cheated the system. Esme had researched Thomas and literally modeled herself into the perfect woman for him. But she'd been unprepared for the commitments that went with being a public servant. She'd thought her life would be all glamorous parties and hanging out with rich people. Instead Thomas had worked eighty-hour weeks, hitting the campaign trail and meeting with voters. He didn't have much time for fancy parties or the money to spend like Esme expected him to.

Esme had set up profiles on most of the higher-priced dating sites, trolling for ways to connect with Thomas and other rich and famous people looking for a partner. It was just a coincidence that Esme was matched with Thomas on Tracy's app.

Esme's roommate was one of those people who did internet sleuthing to find obscure people and dox them. She'd dug through the documents and found out that Tracy was the owner of Fairy Tale Beginnings. The roommate was the one who had been pushing hard for Esme to extort money. Esme had leaked that Tracy owned Fairy Tale Beginnings, thinking that divulging that information would spur the Thayer family to pay out more money by showing that she was serious about revealing their family secrets. She wasn't wrong.

Apparently, Esme had already moved on to someone more interested in publicity than public service.

It frosted Tracy that they had paid her. But the decision had not been hers to make.

Now Bernie said, "We've almost got the right angle to use the opposition research on your father's opponent."

"I think we should just defend the app. I already admitted that I made a mistake." Besides, another story was taking over the news, and the furor around her app and the connection to her father would be dying down.

She was tired of this. And heartsick.

She'd been home for all of a day and she was already fed up with having to watch what she said and what she did.

Not to mention, she had a hangover.

Everything felt off. She felt like her skin was the wrong shape.

She missed Colt.

Bernie wasn't thrilled that she had spoken with the reporter in the bar. "What's wrong with you? We set up the entire spin to take care of the fallout," Bernie chastised her. "I had already prepared a press release and set up a press conference."

"The guy was bothering my...friends."

"You are more savvy than that."

"I was trying to distract him." Tracy hadn't been about to let the reporter near Colt. "So he didn't get close to my friend."

"You should have followed protocol." His next question was cynical. "Besides what friend do you have in Vermont?"

"The people are really nice and welcoming."

"You could charm the stuffing out of anyone."

"I did what I could to protect people who were there for me while I lived in Vermont." She wasn't sorry. She handed him a sheet of cream stationary paper with her resignation on it.

"What is this now?"

"My resignation."

"You're quitting?" Bernie chomped on a cigar, unlit, as he paced around the office. "But, but..."

She wasn't sure she'd ever seen him speechless.

"I have too much going on with my business. Now that my secret is out, I can take a more active role in the day-to-day operations." She had other plans as well, but she was going to discuss them with her parents first.

He snorted. "Matchmaking?"

"Having a healthy, positive, loving foundation is the cornerstone of a stable society." She shoved his spin back at him.

"We can talk about this later."

Which meant he was going to try to talk her out of it. But he was out of luck. She'd made up her mind.

Her dad walked into Bernie's office.

"How you doing, pumpkin?" Most of the time the silly nickname made her smile. Her dad knew she was an adult, but she would always be his baby girl.

She'd been holding it together since she'd returned. But when her dad stepped in to give her a hug, all the pent-up sadness escaped. Her despair bubbled up and she couldn't hold back the sob that erupted from her throat.

"Hold up now. What's this?" Her father squeezed her tighter.

She wrapped her arms around her dad and hung on, tucking her head into the curve of his neck. And she cried.

"Bernie, give us a few minutes," her father said quietly.

"We've got the presser in thirty minutes."

"I might be a few minutes late."

She cried harder.

Because it had been a long time since her father had put her in front of his work.

Tracy cried for her thirteen-year-old self who'd been devastated by the shocking knowledge that her parents' relationship wasn't a fairy tale. She cried for her adult self who had sabotaged several promising relationships to keep her parents' secret safe. And she cried for losing the guy who had gotten her to trust him even while she was holding back. She cried for the loss of Colt. She cried for the loss of Cee-Cee, because she freaking loved her alter ego.

Cee-Cee was the bomb.

"What can I do to help you?" Her father's plea made her cry harder. That's who he was.

"I'm quitting," she said into his now soaking wet shoulder.

"Okay."

Tracy heard her mother come into the room, felt the brush of her hand on her shoulder. "You okay, princess?"

Tracy nodded against her father's shoulder. "I will be."

"That's my girl," her dad's voice rumbled from beneath her ear.

"We are here for you." Her mother's hand on her shoulder felt like acceptance, love.

She was lucky. Her family loved her and supported her. What about all those people out there who didn't have the same kind of support system that she did?

"I'm going to focus more on the offshoot businesses of Fairy Tale Beginnings." The paperwork to create the engagement and wedding planning arms had been filed.

"We are so proud of your accomplishments," her dad said. "But—"

Tracy stepped back from his arms and wiped away the evidence of her tears. "I should have told you about the business."

"Especially since we were blindsided by the news." Her father frowned. "Even so, my opponent was wrong to criticize you."

"Actually, he was correct," Tracy said firmly. "That's the next part of the changes I want to make."

Her mother raised both eyebrows, a small smile playing on her mouth.

"I really had no idea how expensive my registration fee was." Tracy paced around the room. "I'd like to look into either developing a fund that helps people without a safety net or finding existing programs that do just that. And I want the Thayer Family Foundation to put a significant portion of funds into it."

She'd learned a lot by living on a waitress salary for a few weeks and she planned to put that knowledge to good use.

"I was shocked at how little room there was for anything to go wrong," Tracy explained.

Her mother was perfectly made up, wearing a Chanel suit in a pale stem green with nude pumps and matching fingernails. Her makeup was done in coordinating colors. She was the epitome of a perfect political wife.

Maybe her mother had forgotten what life had been like before she'd married her father. And her father had never had to worry about money.

"And it was just for a few weeks. There are people out there living from paycheck to paycheck and one little catastrophe can bring their whole life crashing down on them."

She had listened to her father speak about the average family for years but until she'd actually lived in their shoes she hadn't grasped the fundamentals of how precarious life could be.

She was ashamed of the fact that she'd been trying to dump the foundation business off on Esme.

"What do you need from us?" her mother asked.

"Your support."

"Is that all you want?" Her father raised his eyebrows, knowing that she had more on her mind.

Tracy thought about what she really wanted. To return to Vermont. But that wasn't possible.

"No. But it's a start."

18

COLT

Colt was devastated that Cee-Cee was gone.

He wandered aimlessly around his cabin, thinking up dishes she might like.

He saw an article about strides in gluten-free baking and wanted to talk with her about it. He'd waffled about a little surprise for Chuck and Lottie and wished for her input. He kept finding things he wanted to run past her, business things, couple-y things.

But she was gone.

He see-sawed between anger and anguish. He was a fool to push her away.

Except…he still wasn't sure that he could handle being in the public eye again. He'd seen her father's press conference the other day. She'd been by his side looking amazing.

He'd soaked up how she looked pausing the television to stare at her and see any nuances. She appeared to be a little puffy around her eyes, but maybe he was the only one who noticed.

What he didn't do was reach for the bottle.

He'd been a bear to be around, and he didn't even live with anyone.

He'd spent one night at the Speakeasy moping. Phoebe had commented on his more dour than usual demeanor.

Grace sang a song about love lost that sounded like she was singing just to him.

Matteo had given him a sympathetic look. "Pretty surprising, huh?"

"Yeah." But he'd known her secret was big. The onus was on him as well. He hadn't pushed. Wanting her to keep her privacy. So could he really be upset with her?

Everything reminded him of Cee-Cee, *Tracy*, what he'd lost.

He'd stopped going to the Speakeasy so he'd missed the big to do. Apparently Sam Tremblay and Phoebe had declared their love for each other in front of a crowd. The whole thing was all over social media. Colt was happy for his old friend. But the way they looked at each other, because of course, he'd watched the video, made him miss Cee-Cee even more. And he'd thought she would have loved the public spectacle of it all.

The only constant over the past week was his cooking.

He cooked nonstop as if he were on fire. His brain was constantly bombarded with new ideas and flavor combinations. With every dish, he wondered what Cee-Cee, *Tracy*, would think. And he wished he could get over himself and just call her.

But that would have to wait for another day. He had a fiftieth anniversary party to get ready for.

The Speakeasy staff had taken care of the decorations. Chuck and Lottie hadn't arrived yet, but Colt found himself standing in the middle of the upstairs event room and studying the effect. Everything reminded him of Cee-Cee. *Tracy*, he corrected.

He was sorry she wasn't here to see it.

Crisp white linen tablecloths with centerpieces of white hydrangea flowers in Ball jars spray-painted in gold were simple and cost-effective yet elegant. Mylar heart balloons with Happy

50th Anniversary on them in bunches were tied to the ends of the cake table and the small table up front for the happy couple.

Gold, white, and translucent balloons formed an arch over the gift table, which was scattered with pictures of Chuck and Lottie throughout their life starting with a Polaroid of them on their wedding day looking just as thrilled as they did last week when they'd finalized the menu.

He wanted Chuck and Lottie to be happy with their party, but the success felt hollow without Cee-Cee, *Tracy*, there to celebrate with him.

Colt had spent the day prepping and cooking. He'd used the kitchen on the second floor next to the event space. The kitchen staff had followed his prep instructions easily.

One of the newer staff had messed up. Instead of yelling, he'd patiently explained how he wanted the vegetables chopped and why, and life went on.

No one but him realized that it was a pivotal moment. Cee-Cee. He stopped. Not Cee-Cee. *Tracy* would have known but she wasn't here.

Back in the old days he would have lost his shit and berated the young chef. But his attitude had shifted. He could hear Tracy in his head talking about how the food was meant to be enjoyed and that people didn't need perfection.

The mood in the kitchen was jubilant. The staff danced around each other with a coordinated grace as they chopped and prepped and readied for the anniversary party.

Chuck and Lottie arrived looking ecstatic.

Lottie wore a slim, pale pink beaded dress that hit above her knee, Colt didn't know what the style was called—Tracy would know—Colt just knew she looked radiant. Chuck was in a tuxedo. He appeared supremely uncomfortable. He kept the jacket on for some pictures, but once he removed it, Colt noticed the tape measure hooked to his belt loop.

Their friends and family poured into the Speakeasy and flowed up the stairs. The crowd was eclectic with some attendees coming straight from the farm and still in their jeans and others dressed up as if it were a night out in Boston. They might be dressed differently but they were all happy to celebrate the enormous accomplishment of fifty years of marriage.

The servers walked around with the assortment of specialty sliders and little cups of truffle fries and white napkins with gold script, *Cheers to 50 years, Lottie and Chuck.*

Phoebe had offered several times to take over since the Speakeasy hadn't hired a catering manager yet, but Colt felt extremely proprietary. Every time he dropped in to check the food and see if any tables needed topping refills, someone stopped to compliment him.

After dinner, the toasts started.

Chuck and Lottie's kids each lifted a glass of cider. "Thank you for showing us how to sustain a loving relationship."

"Thank you for being awesome role models."

"Thank you for putting in the work to keep love and romance alive—even if it was embarrassing on occasion."

The crowd laughed.

Someone started dinging their pilsner glass with a spoon, and then the clacking started, and soon everyone was chanting, "Kiss, kiss, kiss."

Chuck and Lottie leaned close and shared a conspiratorial look. They held hands and kissed each other longer than just a peck. The room erupted in cheers.

Then came the calls for them to speak. "Speak, speak!"

Someone tried to hand Colt a glass of cider. He smiled, shook his head, and grabbed a glass of water, feeling blessed to be a part of this beautiful celebration.

Chuck raised his glass. "People said we were too young. It was too fast. But when you know, you know."

Lottie's eyes filled with tears. She mouthed *I love you* at Chuck and they clinked glasses.

They twisted their arms together and tipped back their heads to drink together. The crowd cheered. "To Chuck and Lottie!"

Watching Chuck and Lottie and listening to the stories made him realized that he wanted what they had.

They'd been unbelievably young when they'd eloped.

But through fifty years they'd managed to support each other and stay in love despite the challenges, through hard work and a deep abiding respect and love for each other.

He watched them work the room separately, making sure to talk to every person there.

Lottie, flush with champagne, came over to him. "Thank you so much." She clasped his hand and squeezed.

"My pleasure." And it had been. The couple had been so appreciative. He'd had the chance to stretch his creative muscles. Cooking for Cee-Cee had made him realized that he had lost his joy of cooking long before he lost his restaurants.

And today, his heart was full of happiness for Chuck and Lottie.

"I was wishing Cee-Cee, um Tracy, might be here." Lottie looked sad for a moment.

Him too. There'd been a kernel of hope that maybe she'd remember the date and show up. But Colt was pretty sure she wouldn't. Her presence would distract from the main event and she would never do that to them.

"She sent us the decorations with a note so I was pretty sure she wouldn't make it."

Colt shouldn't be surprised. Even from miles away she was making people happy and spreading her particular brand of joy.

"Can't believe that the famous Tracy Thayer helped plan our little anniversary party." Lottie seemed bemused, then shook it off. "We've got to make sure to take a picture and post it on Fairy Tale Endings' Instagram account."

Tracy's Instagram account?

Except to watch the video of Sam and Phoebe, Colt hadn't been on social media in over a year. He'd eschewed all forms of attention and notoriety when he'd moved to Colebury.

But he wanted what Chuck and Lottie had. He wanted the

whole package. With Cee-Cee, Tracy, whatever she wanted to call herself. But he had to figure out if he could stand to be in the public eye again. "You want to take a selfie?"

Lottie blushed. "With you?"

If he truly was willing to compromise on some things, then this would be a start. He could see if he was ready to step back into the public eye and if he could bear the scrutiny.

"Sure. I'll hold the phone since my arms are longer." Before he could talk himself out of it, he bent to Lottie and smiled for the camera. "Congratulations again." Colt felt a burning need to retreat to the kitchen. What if he'd just made a huge mistake?

Screw it. If he made a mistake, if he fell down, he'd just get back up again.

There was a buzz in the air. It wasn't explicitly about his food, but he was still a part of it.

The message during the party, over and over, was that their marriage hadn't been easy. They'd worked on their relationship. But it had totally been worth it.

"Make sure you get some champagne." Lottie gestured to the long table against the wall with several rows of bottles. "Chuck went a little overboard with ordering. We'll never go through all that." She laughed.

Colt smiled and grabbed a bottle. "I'll bring this to the kitchen staff."

He stuck to water.

He had wondered how he'd do in a stressful situation. If he'd fall back on old patterns and start drinking again. But he hadn't.

He hadn't even been tempted.

A few days later, Colt wandered aimlessly around his cabin. He was miserable. It was too quiet here.

He'd grown accustomed to Tracy's presence. And now that she was gone, he missed her.

Desperately.

Which was insane. He'd only known her for a few weeks. Even the Speakeasy seemed dimmer, less vibrant without her in the space.

He'd been cooking like a madman, testing recipes.

He was pretty sure that his friends were ready to kill him. They'd all commented on his frenetic food production and the fact that he'd posted a picture on social media, but everyone studiously avoided mentioning Tracy.

He'd created ten new recipes this week. He'd dropped off food every place he could think of.

Even at the Three Bears Motor Lodge.

Mrs. Beasley had smiled a thank you and winked at him. "How's our famous resident?"

"No longer a resident."

Her face fell. "That's a shame. She was worth the entertainment. She called me about the crickets one morning, wanting to know if that noise was safe." Mrs. Beasley wheezed, her wrinkled cheeks bunching up as she laughed. "But she made the whole day brighter."

"That she did." Colt forced the words out of tight lips. His heart ached with missing her.

"I recognized her straightaway. Surprised she decided to stay here, so I knew something was up." She tasted the gluten-free coffee cake he'd brought. "This is delicious."

Huh, so Mrs. Beasley had been aware of who Tracy was the whole time.

"After a few weeks, she really started to fit in around here." Mrs. Beasley shook her head. "I tried to steer those reporters away but one slipped through."

A creeping suspicion slithered through his mind. "Was there really something wrong with the pipes?"

She just laughed and then shoved more breakfast cake in her mouth.

TRACY

Tracy shifted restlessly on the fancy upholstered chair at the elegant upscale restaurant while she waited for her brother to arrive.

She looked around and thought Colt would hate this place. Too bland. Too generic. It was the up and coming place to eat but it had no personality. The menu was curated for minimum offensiveness with classic ingredients and recipes that hadn't changed for a hundred years.

Everything was too noisy in the city. She missed the silence of the country. She missed being able to hear herself think.

When her friend Diego had moved from Boston to the Berkshires, she'd thought he was nuts. She knew he loved his girlfriend Penny, but move to the country? He'd done it because Penny's farm was there. She knew he hadn't really had a choice but she had always assumed that he missed city life even though he continued to deny it.

Now she totally understood.

With video conferencing and collaboration software, meetings could take place online. It wasn't imperative to be in the same room as the other meeting attendees. When she'd been working remotely from the motor lodge or Colt's cabin, she'd gotten an incredible amount of work done.

Today was the first time she'd been out of her penthouse in a week. She'd been wandering around her space, wearing her Levi's and Speakeasy T-shirt, and working on creating the company structure for the new spin-offs. But her heart was back in Colebury.

Chuck and Lottie's party had been the past weekend. Tracy had been so tempted to go. She hoped it had been everything that they were expecting.

She scrolled through Instagram on her phone, first checking

the #speakeasy hashtag because apparently she was a glutton for punishment. Seeing the rustic interior and the pictures from happy customers just made her long to be back there. The number one post was a video of Sam and Phoebe that made her heart grow.

She moved on, checking out the posts tagged with the Fairy Tale handles, smiling at the pictures of happy couples celebrating their engagements or weddings.

Until one caught her eye.

Lottie had posted a series of pictures from the anniversary party. Tracy blinked back tears as she looked at the smiling, happy faces. She greedily soaked up the details from the party. Lottie and Chuck looked deliriously happy, all dressed up for the celebration. Platters of Colt's food, the dishes she'd sampled for him, shots of the centerpieces which she had donated, and the gorgeous cake. The final picture was a selfie with Colt and Lottie. It was clear from the picture that he had been the one to snap it.

The lump in Tracy's throat expanded.

He was healing.

A month ago, he was barely comfortable with her showing his hands while she photographed the soup.

She traced the lines of his face with her finger. A million times a day something came across her desk that she wanted to share with him. How could she miss him so much?

Her brother slid into the chair across from her. The table was in the front window. She was sure that was deliberate.

He looked every inch the up-and-coming politician in a navy Brooks Brothers suit with a fine pinstripe, a bright cerulean cotton dress shirt that emphasized the blue of his eyes, and a conservatively striped tie. His clothing not fancy or too expensive, he struck the right note between serious about being a politician for the people but still dressed up enough to respect the office.

"How are you doing?"

This was the first time they had seen each other in person since the whole scandal began. Fortunately, the press had moved on,

Thomas had been able to focus on policy positions and meeting his potential constituents, and Esme was busy filming a reality show where she was isolated for eight weeks.

He shrugged. "I'm fine."

True love was no more? "Getting over your heartbreak?"

He fiddled with his silverware, adjusting the space between the knife and spoon and the edge of the table. "Maybe I wasn't heartbroken."

Tracy blinked.

"I thought I needed a wife to run for office." He looked out the window at the traffic. "She seemed perfect. Too perfect, looking back on it. She never had her own opinions. We never argued about anything."

"Is arguing a requirement for a good relationship?" She and Colt hadn't argued.

"Of course not." He shook his head. "I don't know how to explain it but it was like nothing really impacted her or made her feel. Except maybe when I said I couldn't take her to London for the weekend to see some show. Then she was plenty pissed."

"She didn't share things about her family?"

Tracy wished she'd gotten to meet Colt's sisters and brothers.

"No. She didn't share anything." He clasped his hands together and rested them on the white linen. "Maybe that should have been a big fat clue. She was constantly after *me* to share."

She thought about the give and take between her and Colt and she was sad for Thomas. Her relationship might have been brief but it had been real and intimate and life-changing. "What's next?"

"Definitely not ready to start dating again. I'm going to focus on my campaign."

"Probably a good call." Tracy was happy that her brother seemed to be recovering from the ordeal that had changed her life.

He frowned. "Why are you so sad?"

"What do you mean?"

"Normally you'd already be trying to set me up with someone

new." Thomas shook his head. "I should have realized that Fairy Tale Beginnings was you." He grinned, his bright teeth white in his tanned face, his blond hair swept back from his face.

"Good afternoon. My name is Joy." Their waitress stopped cold and then jerked when she saw Thomas's face. "Can I get water for the table?" she stammered. "Perhaps a spring or sparkling?"

"Tap is fine." Tracy smiled at the girl. "Thank you, Joy."

The waitress recited the specials then said, "I'll be right back with your water."

She and Thomas chatted about mutual friends and the fact that their parents actually seemed to be getting along and spending more time together recently. They talked about everything and nothing until their waitress dropped off their salads.

Tracy glanced around the bright restaurant with its hip décor and slightly pretentious furnishings. She sighed, missing the rustic interior of the Speakeasy.

"What's wrong?"

She missed her customers and the other waitstaff. But most of all she missed Colt. Colt who had clearly made peace with being somewhat in the public eye again since he'd allowed Lottie to post his picture on Instagram.

"I'm fine." *Lie.*

"C'mon. What's going on with you? You don't do depressed." Thomas ate a bite of salad.

She always wanted people to like her. She went out of her way to be perky and bubbly and always upbeat. She didn't do depressed, and she never got mad at anyone even if they deserved it. But since she'd been home it had been harder and harder to maintain that air of bubbly happiness.

"I miss Colebury" was what came out of her mouth. Not the whole truth of course but close.

"That little town you holed up in?" Thomas grinned again. "Really?"

Colt. She wanted Colt. However she could get him. But would he even consider being with her? "I met someone," she confessed.

"In Vermont." Thomas had quit laughing as he finally realized that she was serious. "Well, this is intriguing. When do we get to meet him?"

"He's pretty mad at me right now."

"Who could be mad at you?" Her brother leaned forward, elbows on the table, speaking earnestly. "Your whole life you've been a pleaser. Always looking out for everyone else."

"I lied to him about who I was."

"Lying isn't optimal."

That was putting it mildly.

"Doesn't he understand why?"

She shrugged. "He does. But there are other considerations."

But she thought about Lottie and Chuck and how their message was hard work, stubbornness, and love. She could do all three. And she wanted to do them with Colt.

"You're right," she said.

"About what?"

"It's time for me to please myself," she stated firmly.

"That's not quite what I said." Now Thomas looked alarmed.

But Tracy had made up her mind. "I'm going to tell him how I feel." She was going to go see Colt and tell him. How could she ever expect her own fairy tale if she wasn't willing to fight for it, for them?

19

TRACY

Tracy threw clothes in her weekend bag.

She stood in front of her underwear drawer studying the lace and silk, wondering if she should try to bribe him with sexy underwear.

Oh my God, she was stalling.

But part of her felt as if she needed to get this just right. When they prepped her dad for a press conference, every detail was considered. Colors, lighting, location to make the perfect impact and send the right message.

She had a jittery unsettled feeling as she tried to figure out what to pack.

What in her closet said *I want to move to Vermont and be with you?*

She had no freaking idea. She grabbed the John Deere cap she'd stolen from his cabin and set it on her head. She would only admit in the privacy of her own walk-in closet that she'd worn the stupid thing to bed.

Should she dress casually and wear her Levi's and Speakeasy T-shirt? Remind him of the fun they'd had when she was just plain old Cee-Cee? Or should she dress in her city clothes? Because while she loved living in Vermont, she wasn't actually going to return to waitressing. She was going to be far too busy between the spin-off businesses and her foundation work. Maybe she should dress as she meant to go on, so there wouldn't be any misunderstanding.

And maybe she should see her therapist to discuss why she was having so much trouble deciding on an outfit for the most important conversation of her life.

If he was concerned about her clothing choices, then he wasn't the man for her.

While she continued to waffle, her doorman buzzed her.

She pressed the button. "Yes?"

"There's a Mr. Vega here to see you."

Colt? Here? What did she do with that? She wasn't ready.

"Ms. Thayer?"

Her heart pounded so hard she thought she might be having a heart attack. "Send him up."

She was still in her suit from lunch with her brother, but her feet were bare.

Maybe this was how this was supposed to play out.

Her doorbell rang.

She peered through the security peephole. It was him. Not that she'd thought her doorman was lying but still. She took a deep breath, tried to calm her heart.

He knocked.

Tracy pulled open the door with a flourish. But then words deserted her. He looked…good. Maybe a little thinner. His tan appeared to have deepened. The scruff was missing from his face and his beautiful brown gaze was guarded.

"Hi," she said breathlessly, leaning against the door, and just drinking him in.

He seemed to be doing the same to her, his gaze skimming over her suit and bare feet and then fixating on her head. "Is that…my hat?"

"What?" She flushed. Crap. She'd forgotten she was wearing it. She ripped it off her head and shoved it at him. "Here. You can have it back."

Except his hands were full because he was carrying a dish so he couldn't take it. Tracy whipped it behind her back.

"Are you going to let me in?" There was a lilt of amusement in his voice.

"Oh, yes." She opened the door wider and gestured for him to come inside.

He walked in and stopped, looking around at her penthouse condo. She wondered what he thought of her mix of antiques and more modern furnishings. She had a view of Boston Harbor. It was a far cry from his casual, comfortable cabin.

He paused when he saw the open Louis Vuitton bag. "Are you going somewhere?"

She hadn't had time to plan, to script out what she was going to say. But this was her moment. "Actually—"

"Wait. Never mind." He held up his hand. "It doesn't matter."

He hadn't let her finish. Why didn't it matter?

"I need to tell you something."

"Okay," she said slowly. His solemn expression should have worried her except there was a look in his eyes, a yearning. For her? An unexpected hope beginning to grow in her heart.

"I miss you."

"I miss you too."

"I went to Chuck and Lottie's party," he said haltingly.

"I saw the pictures." She clasped her hands together. She didn't bring up that he'd allowed his face on social media but it was present in her mind. "Was it as wonderful as it looked?"

"Even more so." He began to pace, still holding that dish. "They missed you."

She had wanted to be there, but she hadn't thought that she could handle seeing Colt and she didn't want to take away from their special day.

"At Chuck and Lottie's party, with their happy family around them, raising a glass to their successful relationship, I knew I wanted what they had."

As he spoke, her hope grew. Tracy pressed her hand over her mouth, tears brimming in her eyes.

"With you, in case that wasn't clear," he said when she just continued to look at him with tears in her eyes.

She gave a watery laugh. "I would like that too." That was an understatement. "But we'll have to work out logistics." There was no way she could run the business from the cabin. As much as she loved that space and the time she'd spent with him, she needed more room. Of course maybe she was getting ahead of things. He hadn't asked her to move in with him. She would want to keep the penthouse for when she had to be in the city.

"I know."

She would have to find a place to live in Colebury. Her mind was racing with details. But the one that she kept returning to was that he wanted her.

He wanted her.

COLT

Colt took a deep breath.

"I thought about doing something big and splashy and public to show you what I wanted but then I realized that it would likely need to be run through your father's press office and I know how much you value your privacy. I know you wouldn't want your private business broadcast to everyone."

She looked shocked. "You would have done something like that for me?"

"I would do anything for you."

Truth.

"I listened to Chuck and Lottie's story. They worked on it. That was the message, over and over again. Sometimes life hadn't been easy. It had been messy, and complicated, but they had come through it together. And I realized that I wanted that with you."

She hesitated. "I need to confess something."

His heart stopped.

"I think I'm in love with you."

His heart burst into thunder at her words. She was in love with him.

Before he could say anything, she continued, "I know you don't believe in fairy tales."

"Stop."

Her face whitened. Shit. He was screwing this up.

"You're right. I don't believe in fairy tales. But love, true love is all around us. I believe in love like Chuck and Lottie. It will take work but I'm willing to take that chance."

As if she couldn't believe him, she wrung her hands. "What about the media pressure? Sometimes we'll have to appear at public events. My family isn't just going to go away."

"The past few weeks have been rough." Colt still held onto his pan, like a good luck talisman—he wanted to get out his words and then give her the present. His heart in a dish. "But I didn't reach for a drink. I reached for a whisk."

She laughed again. The most beautiful sound in the world. "A whisk."

"Yes. I've been cooking nonstop." Nothing like heartache to spur a creative frenzy of new dishes.

"That's wonderful."

"I've especially been working on this one recipe. Trying to get it perfect."

He held out the pan.

Now it was her turn to stop him. "Wait."

Wait?

"Don't you want to know where I was going?"

"Not unless you were planning on coming back to Colebury."

"You're in luck. I was coming back to Colebury."

Wait, what? "You were?" He couldn't wrap his brain around her words.

"Yes." She finally took the dish. "To try to convince you to let me come back."

She was blowing his mind right now.

"I...thought you'd want me to move to Boston."

"You were willing to move back here?"

"I'd do anything for you."

"Well, there's a problem," she said.

His heart stopped.

"I don't want to live in Boston anymore." She clutched his pan to her chest. "It's too loud, too chaotic. I'd rather fall asleep listening to the crickets...with you."

"Are you asking me to move in with you?"

"Yes." She held up two fingers in the scout promise gesture. "I promise not to cook for you."

He laughed. "Open your present."

"Ooh. I do love presents."

She took off the lid to reveal a tin full of cinnamon rolls with a thick layer of frosting.

"Cinnamon rolls?" She pulled one from the pan and took a quick bite and hummed in appreciation.

"Gluten-free. I kept tweaking the recipe trying to get it right. But I need a taster. I'm looking for someone who will take care with my heart."

"I've found you a match." Tracy put the pan down and threw her arms around his neck. "If you think you can handle me."

"I can handle anything as long as I've got you in my life."

20

Several months later

TRACY

Tracy glanced out the big picture window in her home office.

Dusk was falling—the November sky a cloudy gray. Flurries swirled in the air and began collecting at the bottom of the white picket fence.

Beyond the fence, the apple and pear trees were bare. To the right of the long drive, long rows of cleared land had been prepped and covered for planting in the spring.

Tracy checked her Cartier watch and closed down her laptop for the night. The Fairy Tale branding decisions could wait until morning.

She and Colt had moved into a larger space—together. The one-room cabin hadn't been big enough for Colt's new venture and her business needs, since she was the CEO and main planner for the wedding offshoot of her Fairy Tale Beginnings business. She'd even launched a division specifically for renewing vows and anniversary parties.

Her life was full and busy. She did occasionally miss Boston, but they'd gone into the city for dinner with the BBC a couple times and of course a few meals with her parents.

She marveled at how much things had changed in the span of a few months.

Colt burst through the front door of their new home. New to them anyway. The hundred and seventy year-old farmhouse was gorgeous with wide planked floors, high ceilings and beautiful crown moldings. It also had drafty windows, an ancient boiler, and appliances from the last century. Everything was functional but they needed to upgrade.

Snowflakes lingered on his eyelashes and in his hair. "I made it before Preston got here."

"Yup."

A local contractor, Preston Kelly specialized in remodeling and restoring historic properties. Tracy wanted Preston even if they had to wait until he had time in his schedule. He was the perfect choice to renovate their big old 1850s farmhouse. They didn't want to lose the charm of the original building, but the kitchen needed to be completely redone to update it with commercial appliances for Colt's new ventures, writing cookbooks under his own name and blending spice rubs and creating sauces for sale. He was specializing in recipes for people with celiac disease.

Colt wrapped her in his arms, lifted her off her feet and twirled her around.

She yelped and then laughed breathlessly. "What was that for?"

"Being your awesome self."

That sounded like he was going to need a favor later. She wrapped her arms around his Canada-goose-covered shoulders and hugged him tight. "Is there something you want from me?"

A heated sensuality lit his deep brown gaze. "I always want somethin'-somethin." He pushed her up against the old pine cabinets and clasped her cheeks in his very cold hands.

"Youch!"

He bent his head. "Don't worry, I'll warm you up," he murmured against her lips.

The moment their lips met, she sighed.

He kissed her like it was the first time. Like he was suffocating and she was air. She melted against him, so much in love with him that sometimes she couldn't believe her good fortune.

She poured her gratitude and love into the kiss, which turned heated in a split second.

She finally pulled away and tried to fluff her hair back into submission.

"Leave it," he said huskily. For him, she would.

"You're always messing me up."

"You're so easy to muss." He teased, but then his face softened. "You're so beautiful."

She shrugged. "Genetics and really expensive facial cream."

"Nope. You are beautiful to the bottom of your soul."

That compliment she would take. He saw her. The good and the bad. And he loved her anyway.

It was the same for her. She saw his commitment every day.

Tracy leaned into his embrace and gave thanks that she'd chosen the Speakeasy all those months ago. "Guess what?"

"Hmm?" He kissed her again.

"Chuck and Lottie agreed to be my first testimonial for Fairy Tale: Happy Ever After...Again."

"Nice. Your Fairy Tale world domination is nearly complete."

She laughed. She didn't want world domination, she just wanted everyone to be as happy as she was.

Colt stripped off his jacket and hung it on a peg in the mud room off the back door.

"How did the interview go?" Colt had agreed to be interviewed by Skye Copeland, who worked at the local television station. He'd been connected with her through Alec's brother, Benito. Colt specifically wanted to raise awareness for philanthropies that tackled childhood hunger and inequalities in the restaurant business. Many people who worked in restaurants were one illness or injury away from disaster.

He grimaced. "It was fine."

Fortunately, after the initial hoopla, the press had left them alone. They had the occasional reporter in town to cover regional news or festivals. Last month the town had been packed for the new Colebury Beer Fest.

"I'm sure you killed it."

"Still not a fan of the press or their questions." But he would do it for a good cause, which impressed the hell out of her.

Tracy and Colt had done a prep session before the interview to get him ready. It was his first public appearance since his meltdown. But living with her, it wouldn't be his last.

Colt grinned. "Answering invasive questions was good practice for Thanksgiving."

Even though the house wasn't ready, they were hosting Thanksgiving for both the Vega clan and Tracy's family.

It would be the first time their families had met. They were both nervous and excited.

Tracy had spent time with Colt's family. She loved the crazy chaos of their get-togethers. Her parents were in for a wild ride because meals with his extended family were nothing like the quiet dinners at their house.

"We're both going to slay Thanksgiving."

Which was good, since she was planning to use the full house madness to put some pressure on her father to change his stance on childcare tax credits.

Although she was working for her Fairy Tale companies full time and no longer involved in the day-to-day dealings of her dad's office, Tracy had used her short experience as a waitress living on a very tight budget to champion for wage equality. She'd convinced her father to change his position on several issues.

She was going to start working on her brother next.

"Already planning your pitch to the newly elected representative?"

"You know it."

Colt tugged her into the living room and onto her favorite French settee, which they'd moved from her condo in Boston. He pulled her onto his lap and nuzzled her neck. "How was your afternoon?"

She leaned against him with a trust that still took her off guard. "I spent the entire afternoon on Zoom meetings and interviews."

The app was going gangbusters. She was planning on taking the company public so that they could change the business model to reach more people. She'd convinced her board to start another offshoot business, childcare for single parents going on dates. They were still working out details, like insurance and what to name that branch.

She was hiring new CEOs left and right to run each individual business, while she retained control over the wedding planning business.

The Thayer Family Foundation had also begun funding for women without a safety net.

They were searching for organizations who would benefit from their grant money. She'd also discussed with her parents that she wanted to direct policy but not run the foundation. They were looking to hire someone to help out her mother, who would ultimately take over the director position so that Tracy could also have a personal life.

Tracy had spent quite a bit of time talking to her mother. She'd never understand her choices, but her mother was happy for Tracy and she'd told her to put her relationship first.

"Don't forget. After our meeting with Preston, we've got dinner at the Speakeasy with Phoebe and Sam and Audrey and Griff."

The doorbell rang.

Colt lifted her to her feet and then headed for their bedroom. "I'll just change out of this suit and be right back."

As the weather grew colder, he'd switched out his cargo shorts and short-sleeved Henleys for jeans and flannel shirts. But he still wore that bit of scruff on his face.

But her absolute favorite outfit was his chef jacket. Every time he wore it, she felt a swell of gratitude and hope for the future. Besides the fact that he cooked incredible meals just for her on a regular basis, he was cooking for himself again. And his vibe was happy and engaged.

Some days she felt as if she were living in a fairy tale.

The kind she'd dreamed of when she was younger. Except now she knew that wasn't quite right.

Because a fairy tale was a fantasy. Falling in love was just the beginning. Working out the kinks in a true relationship took time, effort, compromise. And most of all love.

COLT

A few hours later, a gust of wind ushered them into the Speakeasy.

The blackboard sign at the entrance read: "Life is a one-time offer, use it well."

Kaitlyn, one of the new hostesses, seated them at a table near the stage.

They waved to some regulars at the bar and Tracy told him about her day while they waited for everyone else to arrive.

Watching her talk animatedly, Colt let the swell of love roll through him. The most favorite part of his day was the end when they chatted about what they'd done.

Moving in together full time hadn't been without its challenges. Tracy had more makeup and beauty supplies than all his sisters combined. And she was not neat. Her stuff covered every available inch of counter in the small bathroom.

But he loved to sit and watch her get ready in the morning.

Then once she was all put together, he would frequently tug

her back to bed and proceed to untidy her. Melding their lives had taken compromise on both their parts, but he was one hundred percent all in. He hadn't even thought about a drink or cigarettes. They didn't keep any liquor in the house, but they were frequent patrons of the Speakeasy.

Matteo poured a glass of Sancerre for Tracy and an iced tea for Colt and plopped a lemon in it.

You could take the girl out of France but not the France out of the girl. He was planning to surprise her for Christmas. He'd gotten them tickets to Paris in the spring, and if all went according to plan, he would propose to her at his favorite restaurant.

But that was for the future.

"I had an idea for Thanksgiving. Why don't I see if we can rent the upstairs for our family dinner? There's plenty of space to spread out and I can use their kitchen since ours might be under construction." At last count, they were up to twenty-four people.

"Oh! I love that." She tapped her lips, already planning. "I was going to check with Mrs. Beasley and see if we can put everyone up at the Three Bears."

He wanted to be around for the meeting between Mrs. Beasley and her parents. "That would be…interesting."

"True story." She laughed and changed the subject. "Can't wait to see what Belle has for specials tonight."

While she studied the menu board, Colt took a deep breath. His heart was pounding and his hands were a little unsteady.

He was unaccountably nervous. Maybe he should have done this at home, but he thought that giving her this gift at the Speakeasy was only fitting.

"I have a surprise for you." Not the Paris tickets. Those he would definitely give her in private.

"A surprise," she said slowly.

His girl was not a fan of being surprised but in this case he thought she would be okay. Turned out that planning really was her nature. She liked to be able to consider all the different angles of a situation before making a decision.

Becoming Cee-Cee had allowed her to relax some, but she couldn't completely turn off that part of her personality.

"I got the mock-up of the labels." Colt had been developing recipes for gluten-free savory and sweet sauces and luxurious spice rubs with exotic ingredients based on his travels and kitchen experiences.

He had also expanded his garden, digging larger plots to plant vegetables and herbs for test recipes. Whatever he didn't use would go to Noah at the food bank. It was win-win for everyone.

He handed her the envelope with the sample labels.

He loved how they turned out.

She pulled them out of the envelope, then raised her gaze to his. "Cee-Cee's Kitchen?"

He'd thought long and hard about names and meanings and his life's purpose. "Yes."

He loved everything about the labels. The graphic designer had created a logo depicting a small whisk topped with a princess crown and leaning against a larger whisk wearing a chef's jacket and toque.

"But...I don't cook."

"If Cee-Cee hadn't come along, neither would I."

She was already shaking her head. "You would have gotten back in the kitchen eventually."

He wasn't so sure.

Now Colt was still catering some events but as the business grew, people were bringing in their own chefs. Word was, Alec had a line on a catering manager. Which thrilled him. He'd done a few client meetings but they definitely were not his forte.

He hadn't completely changed and sometimes he had to dig deep to find his patience.

Colt reached for her hand and laced their fingers together. He brushed a kiss over her knuckles. "Cee-Cee gave me the impetus to start living again."

"I'm so grateful every day that I decided to stop in Colebury."

"Best decision ever." A little over a year ago he'd been at rock bottom. Sick and sick at heart and he'd stayed that way, a grumpy hermit who had no desire to wander outside his small existence. Until this crazy, sweet, big-hearted woman had stopped in the Speakeasy—by chance—on the same afternoon as him and somehow burrowed into his life.

She was nothing like his first impression. "I love you."

She flushed. Like she did every time he said it. As if she still couldn't believe it. He would spend every day of the rest of his life proving to her how much he loved her.

"I love you too," she said softly, love shimmering in her blue eyes.

"Our life might not be fairy tales and roses and woodland animals singing but—"

"It's perfect," she defended hotly.

"It's perfect for us."

THE
END

ACKNOWLEDGMENTS

Thank you to Sarina Bowen for allowing me to participate in the True North world. Working on the Speakeasy series has been so much fun.

Thanks as always to Deb Nemeth for being an awesome editor!

Thanks to the BBB for our weekly motivational sessions. I am grateful to have you in my life.

Thanks to my family. I love you all.

Last, but not least, thanks to Jane, Jenn, and Natasha at Heart Eyes Press for the information and guidance. You are awesome.